Sex & Violins

An Erotic Crime Anthology
Edited by Sandra Murphy

****

Misti Media LLC

Also Edited by Sandra Murphy

Chris Bauer likes his stories short and furnished with twists and turns readers won't see coming.

Those in this collection range from out-of-control Thanksgiving turkeys to a bomber pilot's fateful flight, and take the reader from a pizza delivery joint to a homemade backyard rocket ship.

Even his machines seem to have minds of their own, with a love for pranks — or even more deadlier plans.

But, if you're lucky, sometimes serendipity solves the problem.

And let's face it, whichever way you serve it, Revenge is *always* sweet. Unless you're a squirrel. In which case it's just plain nutty.

So, sit back and enjoy a variety of locations, plots, and an introduction to some of the very strange people and the worlds they live in.

Paperback ISBN: 9781963479348
eBook ISBN: 9781963479331

Sex & Violins

An Erotic Crime Anthology
Edited by Sandra Murphy
First published by White City Press
An imprint of Misti Media LLC
https://www.mistimedia.com
Available in both Paperback and eBook Editions
1 2 3 4 5 6 7 8 9 10
Copyright © Respective authors 2024
Ebook ISBN: 9781963479560
Paperback ISBN: 9781963479577

This is a work of fiction. The characters, dialogue and events in this book are wholly fictional, and any resemblance to companies and actual persons, living or dead, is purely coincidental

Contents

Introduction

Welcome to the dark side where anything goes between consenting adults.

They say an orgasm is a 'small death'. For those characters in the stories that follow who take advantage of their tryst partners, who toy with the feelings of others, who think their pleasure is all that matters—well, we can only hope they enjoyed the 'small death' because it's guaranteed, they won't enjoy the real one. The fun of this anthology is in showing how there isn't always a happy ending to a fun night of "Netflix and Chill."

Sex & Violins had challenges on its path to publication. In the edit stage at a previous publisher it was abruptly cancelled. Then resurrected. And cancelled again. You can't keep a good anthology down for long though, and it finally came together at Misti Media under their White City Press imprint. It's been a blast discovering how different authors approached the anthology idea of combining music and sex. Now that the book is complete, and now that I've read forty or fifty potential erotic stories, written one, and then edited the final twelve multiple times, everything sounds dirty.

In my other life, I write magazine articles, edit a newsletter, write short fiction where people may die but with their clothes on. There are at least four books in varying degrees of doneness and many short stories inhabiting my hard drive. Yet, the characters I created for my contribution to this anthology have really stuck with me. They might just have to show up in future stories.

Many thanks for the writers who had the patience to stay with me through all the ups and downs, and many thanks to all of you readers who support unusual anthologies and the small presses that publish them. Your support makes us tingle in all the right places.

Sandra Murphy

September 2024

A Legacy for Murder
Jack Bates

The posters outside the Pinnebog Opera House heralded the limited engagement of mezzo-soprano Rachel McKinnon. Below her picture, in a smaller, finer print, it mentioned we, the Port Pinnebog Symphony Orchestra, would accompany her. Not that I objected to the lesser billing though some did. Personally, I didn't understand why. To have an internationally recognized vocalist appear with us was just the kind of booster shot our ailing community needed. In the decades since the shipping industry abandoned Port Pinnebog, a once vibrant city along Michigan's thumb coast, it had slowly rusted away. We needed Rachel McKinnon. She was, after all, a triple threat.

Hell of a voice.

Hell of a presence.

Hell of a body.

When she sang, it was like only two people were in the theatre: her and you.

I was part of the orchestra's four-man percussion section. Earl Bailey handled the timpani. Paul Clayton smashed the cymbals or plinked the triangle. AJ Peterson clapped or shook or struck specialty rhythm corps items like the claves or the hyoshigi, a Japanese version of clapping sticks. Sometimes called kabuki clappers, musicians use them to make snapping or cracking sounds from a pair of thick, bamboo blocks connected by a red and gold striped cord a foot and a half long. Usually, they were used in holiday songs like 'Sleigh Bells' or any cinematic cowboy score.

Or, in this case, murder.

As for me, I was the vibraphonist. Most people think of a vibraphone as a rolling xylophone with hanging pipes. If anything, it's closer to the marimba, which I play at times. The vibraphone has steel keys that are tuned on a regular schedule. Those hanging pipes are resonators. A foot pedal allows the vibraphonist to create the right amount of tremolo.

Apparently, I was giving it too much.

Leonard Vincent, our conductor, shook his head in his usual overly dramatic manner. His face puckered as if he'd sucked a lemon, seeds and all. He waved his hands over his head and swished his baton like a miniature ninja sword. The orchestra lowered its instruments as it was impossible to follow Vincent's erratic direction.

"No, no, no," Vincent moaned. He directed his ire at me. "Listen to me, Reynolds. The final movement is a soothing rain, not a bloody thunderstorm. How many times must I remind you? Softly taper to a single, final note followed by silence."

"You know, Marty," Earl Bailey said. "Diminuendo." He mouthed 'soft', then lightly drummed the toms atop the brass kettles. As usual, he offered his smart-ass grin.

As usual, I offered him my middle finger. A ripple of laughter echoed around the stage. Leonard Vincent was not amused. He turned to Rachel McKinnon, who sat on a stool nearby.

"Miss McKinnon." Vincent bowed slightly. "Allow me to apologize for the immature behavior of my orchestra."

McKinnon smiled. Like Vincent's anger, the smile was directed at me. "Oh, it's okay, Maestro. You know musicians."

"Musicians, yes." Vincent left it at that. He did not try to mask his disdain for our section.

We ran a couple more of her selections. Vincent found others to fault. He didn't want to say what we were all thinking: Rachel McKinnon was phoning it in. Vinnie took it out on us. Everyone knew she was doing us a huge favor. No need to make a scene that might upset her, even if it upset the people he worked with every day.

"If you want to know what I think," a voice from the back of the house announced. We became attentive, professional even, at the sound of it. No one knew she would be there, but we weren't at all surprised she was. Janet LeMerise was the orchestra's largest benefactor.

She stood at the bottom of the stage, a sophisticated woman in her forties whose eyes forever said, 'Do. Not. Cross. Me. Ever.'

"I think Miss McKinnon knows her voice better than any of us. I think she's preserving it by reserving it."

"The benefit is in two days," Vinnie said quietly.

Her laugh was mirthless. "Oh, relax, Leonard. What's the old adage? 'Bad dress rehearsal, great opening night.' My God. The only groups more superstitious than athletes are performers." We laughed with her. "Go out. Go home. Go away from here. Don't worry about Len. He agrees, don't you, Leonard?"

Vinnie smiled at his music stand. "Of course." He looked up and he looked tired. "Horns are down."

The usual commotion followed as we packed up for the evening.

"Leonard?" Janet LeMerise said. "May I see you?"

Paul Clayton looked back over his shoulder. "What do you think that's about?"

"Maybe it's his turn," Earl Bailey said.

"Would ya?" I asked.

AJ Packer smiled. "Would and have."

After the particularly stressful rehearsal, the guys and I retired to our favorite haunt, the Taconite Lounge, a dive bar on the north end of Main. It used to be popular with freighter crews during the city's boom as a shipping port for taconite pellets, an essential component in manufacturing steel. Walk in any time of the day and catch a whiff of stale smoke and sour beer. Maybe a hint of sailor. Maybe a waft of the past rising through the trapdoors of the rum-running tunnels that crawl beneath the brick buildings along Main. Most of the traffic the Tac gets now is from locals on pub-crawls or drunken college students who come in for what they think is taco night.

The guys and I dropped quarters into a Phantom of the Opera

themed pinball machine. I was working the flippers, trying to get the chandelier to drop for the bonus score when AJ shifted his weight away from the wall.

"You've got to be shitting me," he said and looked toward the door.

I didn't need to turn around to see what AJ saw. Mirrors advertising Port Pinnebog Pale Ale on either side of the pinball machine allowed me to see Leonard Vincent come in with Rachel McKinnon and other members of the orchestra, one of which was Lacy Zhu, a violinist I dated on and off. More off than on, actually. Lacy pointed at us. The entourage made its way to our corner.

Paul Clayton leaned back in his chair. "Of all the gin joints, eh AJ?"

AJ scoffed, then moved to the game.

"What's with him?" I asked.

Paul smirked, shrugged.

Lacy was all smiles and stumbles. "Sorry, boys. We're crashing your party."

"Miss McKinnon wanted a place with atmosphere," Vincent said.

Earl Bailey belched. "That should raise the barometer." We percussionists laughed like it was some kind of inside joke when, in actuality, it was just Earl's way of telling the interlopers to take a hike.

No such luck.

The tables at the Taconite were square four-tops. Vincent pulled two additional tables next to ours. That made us a party of ten. I sat at the end nearest the pinball machine; Vincent took the seat at the other end. Lacy was next to Earl. Rachel McKinnon was on Vincent's left. AJ and Paul had the machine. The rest of the party filled in the empty chairs.

A waitress in skinny jeans and a pink tee shirt with 'It's Taconite' on the front and 'Not Taco Night' on the back came over to take our order. Vincent asked for a wine list.

The waitress held her round tray over her belly like she was hiding behind it. "We have red. We have white. We have pink."

Earl and I stifled laughs. Lacy rolled her eyes. The others looked about uneasily. Vincent fidgeted with the gold, diamond-chip, signet ring on his right hand, something he did when he was frustrated. McKinnon stepped in to save him.

"How about a round of Screaming Tarantulas?" McKinnon swung her hair back revealing how her long, strong throat rose from the plunging V-neck of her red, sleeveless top.

The waitress, uncertain of the cocktail, asked, "What's in it? In case Joe at the bar asks."

McKinnon smiled. "Two fingers tequila, one finger triple sec, finish with lemonade. Salt the rim."

Two rounds later, the edge was off the group. Conversations and drinks flowed. An uninhibited Vincent couldn't stop telling Rachel McKinnon his theories on music. No one else could get a word in the conversation, prompting them to splinter off on their own topics.

It had to be tediously dull. Since her arrival three days prior, Vinnie had been a constant companion to McKinnon. A welcoming dinner with the symphony board. A luncheon with Janet LeMerise. Dinner with patrons of the Port Pinnebog Arts Council. Through it all, there was Vinnie. He was not leaving a good impression.

"Look at Leoncavallo's 'Pagliacci' or Verdi's 'Otello'. It becomes obvious…"

McKinnon finally stopped Vinnie by taking his hand. "That's an unusual ring."

"It's called the Legacy Ring," Vincent said. "I never take it off. It's been passed along from each previous conductor to the next for one hundred years. The Legacy goes all the way back to the founding maestro Leonard somebody…wait! I'm Leonard somebody." Vincent found this more amusing than the people around him did.

The waitress returned. "Another round?"

"Yes! Yes! A thousand times yes!" Vinnie slapped a hand on the table. McKinnon jumped. "What did you call those drinks?"

"A mistake…Screaming Tarantulas."

AJ and Paul finished their set on the machine. Earl fell into a deep, philosophical discussion with Lacy regarding the pandemic's long-term effect on the arts.

"Any challengers?" I held up two quarters.

"I'll take you on," Rachel McKinnon stood quickly.

Vincent tried to stand with her. "Yes! Pinball! What better way to show how sound manipulates mood —oh…" He wobbled a bit.

AJ was there to redirect Vincent. "What are you talking about, Maestro?"

"I was telling Miss McKinnon—" Vinnie gave him a wry smile. He wagged a finger at AJ. "You left the kabuki clappers out again, didn't you?"

"Did I?"

To prove his point, Vinnie fumbled in his pocket and produced the rope-bound clappers. "Guilty!"

"You couldn't just…"

At the pinball machine, McKinnon whispered, "Your friend is a hell of a wingman."

"Trust me. AJ's not just doing it to help me. He's taking notes to be used later."

"Not a fan of the Maestro?"

"He's not alone. You want first ball?"

McKinnon laughed. "We still talking about the game?"

I flashed a grin. "I can see how that might be misleading."

She spread her hands along the metal edging and leaned forward over the flashing lights and ringing bells beneath the glass. She leaned just far enough to allow her cleavage the opportunity to say, 'Look at me!'

Behind us, Vinnie stewed. I had put a wedge between him and McKinnon.

"I better let you go first," McKinnon said.

"Pinball virgin?"

She bumped her hip into mine. "Step aside, drummer boy. And get ready to pay."

"We putting money on this?"

"Unless you can think of other stakes." McKinnon raised an eyebrow.

We played until the banter reached the fork that divided into two paths: Screw or Screw Up. We came up with a plan to leave under the pretense of getting Vincent home. It would require AJ's assistance. In the end, we probably fooled no one but four of us left together. AJ and I walked Vincent out of the bar while McKinnon held the door.

Out on the sidewalk, I thanked AJ. "I owe you, Big Man."

"Trust me, Marty, I'll collect that debt."

We lowered Vinnie onto a bench. "We good?"

AJ nodded. "Yeah. Go on. Get out of here. I've got this." He brought out his phone.

I wandered to the corner where McKinnon waited.

"Not the smoothest exit," I said.

"I've had rougher."

"I guess we could have used the tunnels."

"Tunnels? What? You're a community of preppers and everyone has a go-bag stashed in their trunk?"

"Yeah, that's us."

McKinnon laughed. "You're serious."

"Back during Prohibition bootleggers dug tunnels under the buildings to bring in Canadian booze. There's a trap door in every cellar floor that opens onto an oval rail track. Each train had two flatbeds and a hand pump car."

"You're making this up."

"Swear to God. They paid guys to hand pump the trains around the loop."

"That's a hell of a lot of hand pumping."

"Well, women wouldn't arrive here until after the Volstead Act was repealed so go figure."

She laughed and we stopped to stare at each other, then held one another as we kissed. A car raced past and someone yelled 'get a room'. We both thought that was a good idea. She didn't want to go back to the Port House Inn so I took her to my bungalow where we could at last explore our desires.

With the window open, we moved to the steady rumble of waves along the beach. The cool night air off Wolfhead Bay and the heat of our passion aroused us both. Our bodies jumped at that first naked contact. Flesh to flesh. Entwined. Guiding me into her warmth, she straddled me. I felt the tremor of excitement in her thighs as she rose and fell. I raised my hips to push deeper into her lust and when at last I cupped her breasts and rolled my tongue over her nipples, she cried out, "Yes, yes, oh, yes!" until we climaxed in one grand crescendo.

I was still in the position of immense fulfillment when McKinnon began to dress. Her actions surprised me, so I began to dress, too.

McKinnon laughed. "What are you doing?"

"I'm not letting you walk back to the Port House alone."

"I'm just going out for a smoke."

"Your voice. Smoking can't be good for it."

"Yeah, well, no voice lasts forever."

A crescent moon floated high over Wolfhead Bay. Stars littered the sky. McKinnon sat cross-legged in an Adirondack. I slacked in a similar chair. A stone fire pit waited at our toes. We could see the bay and the orange-ish glow of pole lights along the wharf. A freighter sailed by, the hum of its engines resonating like a low octave C over the waves of water and sound.

"This is a nice place." She lit a cigarette. After a long inhale, she jetted smoke that snagged on the lower tip of the c-shaped moon.

"Yeah. Small but a nice fit for a percussionist. Used to be Cabin Eight of a twelve cabin resort."

"Went out of business?"

"You could say that. Owner got busted for running the place as a brothel."

She offered me the cigarette, but I refused. She felt the need to defend her actions.

"I'm not a habitual smoker, Marty. An occasional cigarette won't do much damage. It won't be long before I go from bad girl roles in operas to torch singer in resort lounges. I mean, I'm twenty-seven. I can already feel my hardened edge soften. If I had gone off to Broadway, my career would be done."

"Is that why you're here? Testing the tour waters?"

She shook her head as she inhaled. Smoke came out in puffs as she spoke. "No. Kind of. Yeah, I guess. It's part of a non-profit organization. Opera-Ation Nation. The goal is to introduce opera around the country. A week here, then I'm off to Milwaukee before I go back to the Met to rehearse for the fall season."

"Busy girl."

She reached over with her free hand and stroked my arm. "Maybe you can come see me. I'm in an experimental adaptation of Lear. It's set during Prohibition."

"Which of the sisters are you?"

"Goneril."

"You mezzos really prefer the wicked roles, don't you?"

"Soprano roles tend to be flat and one-dimensional. Perfect for an ingénue. All innocent and doomed. Playing the villain is always more interesting."

We both heard a snap behind us.

McKinnon stubbed out the cigarette in the sand. "What was that?"

"Not sure." I sat up and turned to look at the trees near the cabin. "Someone there?"

No one responded.

"Maybe it was an animal…" McKinnon said, as if asking for reassurance.

"Could have been anything from a possum to a bear. You don't have a stalker, do you?"

"Do you?"

I thought I saw something move behind the evergreens. I convinced myself it was just the Thuja trees moving in the breeze off the bay.

"We should go inside."

"Bears. Hookers. Stalkers. Hell of a town."

A stronger, chillier wind blew off the bay. McKinnon shivered.

"Come on," I said. "Let's go."

McKinnon attempted to make the situation lighter. "Tomorrow we have late rehearsal. Maybe after breakfast you can show me around town."

"You've already seen the Tac…"

We joked but she clutched my arm on the short walk back to the cabin. I didn't know about her, but I couldn't shake the feeling we were being watched. Sleep was a welcomed comforter.

The sun rose over Wolfhead Bay, casting its reflection across rippling waves. Dark clouds crept in from the west. I had lived in Huron County long enough to see summer mornings darken like February evenings. The day would be overcast and misty. I expected fog.

McKinnon slept as I slipped out of bed. I wanted to poke about the trees next to the cabin. I didn't expect to find the imprint of a shoe or boot. The sand was too soft to produce that. Shallow craters often remained from where someone stepped or stood. I found no indication of it. What I did find was a myriad of broken sticks, but it was impossible to ascertain when they were broken or what did the breaking.

"Lose something?"

McKinnon stood on the stoop outside the door. The tee shirt she'd taken from the shelf left her ass partially exposed. I abandoned my investigation to have breakfast in bed with her, though neither of us brought any food.

I took her for an actual breakfast at the ill-named Bayview Diner. The only view it offered was the northeast end of Main Street.

As we sipped second cups of coffee, we saw a frantic Leonard Vincent bang his fist on the dark, glass door of the Taconite Lounge. He was still there when McKinnon and I hurried from the diner, though by then he paced in front of the bar as he spoke into his phone. He saw us and put it in his pocket. Our presence didn't appear to reassure him.

"Something wrong, Leonard?" McKinnon folded her arms over her chest.

He held up the back of his right hand. "I can't find the Legacy ring. Woke up and it was gone."

"You think you left it at the Tac?" I asked.

"I never take it off, Reynolds. Jesus! You know that."

"Do I?"

McKinnon tried to keep us focused on the current problem. "Maybe it slipped off."

"You know what I think? I think someone took it."

I scoffed. "Right off your hand."

"Yes."

"And you didn't notice?"

"Maybe you forgot we'd all been drinking."

"Blackouts are your demons, Vinnie. Not mine."

"AJ called for a ride," McKinnon said. "Maybe you left it in the car."

Vincent shook his head. "You mean Earl."

"AJ and Marty carried you out to the bench. AJ waited with you."

"All I remember is Earl Bailey helping me into a car."

"Where was AJ?"

Vinnie's only response was a wide-eyed, 'I don't know' shake of his head. He pulled his phone from his pocket and wandered back to the Tac's door.

"Dumb luck, Vinnie." Although luck might not have been the word I used.

McKinnon nudged me in the ribs. "I don't think he heard you."

I caught her elbow. She tried to pull away. Her arm twisted a bit and she complained I hurt her. I released her.

I showed her all the quaint shops, the historic locals, and the library built like a castle. McKinnon seemed less receptive. Her mood chillier. We walked along the back of the L-shaped breakwater and passed Paul Clayton on his way back to shore. He carried a fishing rod and tackle box but no fish.

"Not biting?" I asked.

Paul shook his head. "A few tugs. Nothing more. Fog's getting too thick to be out there."

"So, you guys close the Tac last night?"

"Nah. Party broke up after you all split. Earl left with Lacy. That left me with the Zhu Crew and you know what party animals they are."

They weren't. Paul and I made explosion sounds and each spread the fingers on one hand simulating fireworks. We whistled softly, trailing off.

"They a thing now?" I asked. "Earl and Lacy?"

Paul shrugged, winked. "You just never know with those two."

"Hey. Did you see them give Vinnie a ride?"

"Those two? No. But you know who did show up? Lady LeMerise."

"What was she doing there?"

Paul shrugged. "Maybe AJ called her. All I saw was her Mercedes. I didn't see her. Anyhow, I've got to roll. Watch your step out there, you crazy kids."

After Paul left, McKinnon asked, "Does that bother you? Lacy leaving with Earl?"

"No. Why should it?"

"Lacy told me you two dated."

"That was a while ago. What else did she tell you?"

"She said you have a temper."

"I don't have a temper."

"Then what's your problem with Leonard Vincent?"

"I don't—"

"Come on, Marty. Everyone sees it. Yesterday you were goading him. Today you would've brushed him off if I hadn't been here. What does everyone have against him?"

"He doesn't know music. He's—he's Harold Hill but he believes in the Think Method. Do you know why he was named conductor? Gustav Shafer, the guy before him, wanted to boot him from the orchestra but Janet LeMerise went to the symphony's board of directors and threatened to pull her endowment unless the board dumped Maestro Gustav."

"Politics in the arts? Say it ain't so, Joe."

I snapped and said a little too loudly, "Janet LeMerise is Leonard Vincent's aunt."

McKinnon looked about sheepishly. "Okay. Okay. I get it. Your line in the sawdust is nepotism. Good thing you don't have a temper."

I felt terrible and frustrated. I tried to apologize. "Rachel. I…"

"Listen. I would like to go back to the Port House and take a shower. Why don't we rendezvous at the opera house at three and you can show me the tunnels before rehearsal, okay?'

"I—"

She put her finger to my lips. "I'll see you at three," she said. Her hand dropped. She leaned forward and kissed me.

I watched her walk away.

I wanted to go after her. She had her phone to her ear, which said to me she needed space. What she said about how I treated Vinnie or Lacy or Earl or anyone I had a low tolerance for didn't exactly cast me in a positive light. A dreary realization overwhelmed me. When the week concluded, McKinnon would move on to Milwaukee. I would more than likely never see her again. I knew—I just knew if I ever hoped to avoid that fate, I needed to amend my behavior.

I went back to the Taconite Lounge to see if Vinnie was still there. The guy behind the bar looked up from his phone. "Get you something, bud?"

"I'm looking for a friend. He thought he might have lost a ring here last night."

The bartender pulled up a cardboard box from under the back counter and set it on the bar in front of me. "No one here when I opened. This is our Lost and Found."

I looked but didn't see the ring.

Outside, I tried to call Vinnie. Each time it went straight to voice mail.

I got the same response when I called AJ. I left him a message, asking what happened with Vinnie the night before.

I headed to AJ's apartment, over his music shop on Main. The sign on the door was flipped to 'Sorry, We're Closed'. AJ sat in his office. He removed a pair of noise-deafening headphones when he saw me.

"I didn't miss a rehearsal, did I?"

"No. You talk to Vinnie today?"

AJ shook his head. "Not since last night. Why?"

"I thought you were calling him a ride?"

"I was going to, but he said he wanted to go back in and talk to that waitress."

"Did he?"

"I told him it was a bad idea. He went off on me about never putting away the smalls. Sonofabitch pulled the kabuki clappers out of his pocket and swung them like nunchucks. I was done after that. Last I saw him, he went back into the Tac."

"You didn't take the ring, did you?"

"No, but I know who has it."

"Wouldn't by any chance be Janet LeMerise, would it?"

"Yeah, but how did you know?"

"Paul said he saw her car out in front of the Tac. She doesn't strike me as someone who cruises dive bars after midnight."

"How do you think I hooked up with her?"

"So you went home with her last night?"

"Actually, we went back to my apartment. I may have told her a few things about Vinnie."

"Whew, I can think of better ways to seduce someone."

"We talked after. Anyhow, she said she'd take care of it."

"So, Vinnie didn't lose the ring, he surrendered it."

"That would be my guess."

Vinnie's office door was locked. He hadn't returned my phone call. Short of going to his house, all I could do was wait to see him at rehearsal.

I went down the stairs from the third-floor offices to the gilded and opulent lobby. The curtain for Aisle Two was pushed back to reveal the thick, soundproof double doors to the theater were open.

Leonard Vincent stood on the stage conducting an orchestra of phantoms. It appeared to be a private performance for the lone person front row center.

Janet LeMerise.

Even from the back of the house I could tell something wasn't right. I mean beyond the shadow conducting. The way LeMerise's head lolled to the right but didn't move. The closer I got, the more I realized it would never move again. Wrapped around her neck, like an elegant garrote, was the kabuki clapper.

"Martin." Vinnie stood at the lip of the stage and stared down at me. "Do you know what the loudest moment of any orchestral movement is?"

I didn't answer.

Vinnie closed his eyes and smiled as if he heard. "The loudest moment is the silence."

Leonard Vincent walked across the stage the way he would if the spotlight followed him. Proud. Determined. Grateful for the admiration. I couldn't tell what he was saying but it looked as if he were thanking the only person in the audience for attending his final performance. He made his way down the wing steps to the seats where he removed the signet with a diamond chip in it from his pinkie finger, placed it in the palm of his dead aunt's cold hand, and closed her lifeless fingers around it. He kissed the hand before he headed up the center aisle.

McKinnon passed him at the door. "Oh, hey, Leonard. Did you ever find your ring?"

"My aunt has it."

McKinnon watched him leave. "What's with him?" McKinnon asked me. I was on my phone, explaining the situation to a deputy sheriff and then McKinnon knew. Pretty soon all of Port Pinnebog knew.

A tradition ended when Vincent walked out of the theater. A ring that once had a legacy of honor now had a legacy of murder.

Winter Performance
Laura Hazan

Anna dashed up Charles Street as soon as she hung up the phone. Little-Staten, the head of security at the symphony hall, had called to inform her about a death and police activity. She crossed the intersection and counted at least six emergency vehicles. The most concerning was, of course, the coroner's van. With the hall's emergency exits and front doors splayed open, she could darn near see through to the stage.

The administrative staff gathered near the ticket office window. Anna rushed toward them. "Who can give me current information? Do we know who's dead?"

A few "Good morning, Maestro," along with explanations of gas leaks, robbery, and murder came at her all at once.

She pulled her sweater, inadequate for a December morning, a bit tighter. "Murder?"

The ticket office manager grabbed Anna's arm and guided her away from the group. "We don't really know what happened but they keep saying library, librarian, stuff like that. Sue thought she heard the word murder and now she can't think of anything else."

"I saw David in the library last night when I returned bowings to him. I'd approved them for the Solstice Concert next week, he wanted them right away. Less than twelve hours ago." Anna's voice began to quiver but she cleared her throat. She'd let no one even glimpse a crack in her facade.

Henri, her administrative assistant, approached. "We're all distressed, Maestro. It's okay to cry." He tried to put his arm around her.

She shrugged him off. "I'm not crying, Henri. Must you always be so dramatic?"

Anna, the conductor for the Baltimore Symphony, had known David for years. He was the symphony librarian, a highly specialized position which worked side-by-side with the conductor. They collaborated on every performance. He knew her baton movements intimately. That's the way any orchestra librarian succeeded in their work. The librarian sat in rehearsals and noted, adjusted, and tracked the music for each instrument and the conductor. Anna and David had a relationship her colleagues envied. She gave him her best, and he accepted it as a caretaker. She didn't even want to envision any harm had come to him.

Henri motioned to the left. A detective and Little-Staten stopped at the group of employees, said a few words, and then came toward Anna and Henri.

Tall, easily over six feet, the detective had a classic television cop look. A cheap suit hung off him like it had never seen the inside of a dry cleaner. Stern eyes betrayed his warm smile, as if he'd been instructed to be approachable but hated it.

"Maestro," Little-Staten began, "This is Detective Murphy. I knew him in my years with the Baltimore Police Department. He's tough but thorough and fair. He's requested to speak to you. I agreed to make introductions."

"Pleasure to meet you, Ms. Small." He extended his business card.

Henri leaped between them. "She is the Maestro, please address her properly, especially in her concert hall."

Anna took the card, then put her hand on Henri's arm. "It's okay. Very few outside our circles know how to address a conductor." Her gaze returned to the detective. "Can you tell us what's going on?"

"I have some questions for you, Ms. Small. Maestro. I'd like you to come inside," Murphy said.

Henri made himself as large as possible for a man of small stature. It was his nature to be protective, especially with Anna. "Does she have to go with you? Can't you ask your questions right here? Maybe she should have a lawyer."

Little-Staten stepped beside Henri. "She's in safe hands. This is standard procedure, nothing to worry about. Everyone will be interviewed."

"I'm certain the Maestro would prefer we chat in private," Murphy added.

Anna turned to Henri. "It will be fine. You go with Lolita and gather any questions the rest of the staff may have, make a list in order of priority. I want to see it when I'm done with Detective Murphy." Henri needed a specific task to accomplish so he could maintain his deportment.

"I don't like this at all, Maestro. I am here if you need me."

Detective Murphy led Anna toward the gaping emergency exit. She'd had little time to dress for the weather or the stature of her position. It didn't please her to be in jeans, a turtleneck, and a sweater with her hair in a topknot but maybe it was okay once in a while to let the staff know she was human.

She was tiny next to Murphy, her petite frame barely came up to his shoulder. She changed her guess about his height, he was well beyond six feet. Anna was attracted to tall men. Under other circumstances, she might have even flirted with him.

They entered the concert hall. Swarms of first responders packed up their gear, talked on phones, or stood at the box office counter and wrote—notes, reports, letters—she wasn't sure. She couldn't reconcile this flurry of official activities with the festive trees, wreaths, garlands, and gold trimmings in the lobby. Murphy directed her toward the auditorium.

"I have an office suitable for this," she said without breaching the threshold. "What are all of these people doing in my concert hall?"

"Your concert hall? You mean the symphony's concert hall."

"I am the symphony." Anna turned and strode toward the administrative offices, not giving Murphy a choice about the location to talk.

However, as they walked toward her office, she agreed he could record the interview since there'd be no other witnesses. The conductor's suite, tucked on the third floor, was the largest in administration, of course. Anna flipped on the lights. She knew it didn't look like any office Murphy had ever seen. More practice space than business-like, a grand piano, an assortment of brass and string instruments, and a couple of conference tables spread with sheet music filled the outer room.

"My office is through here." Anna pointed toward a door.

Murphy pulled out a chair next to a conference table. "I think this is private enough."

She plunked her bag next to the piano. "As you wish." Anna took the seat across from him.

The detective started with devastating news. "Mr. Mendoza, the librarian is dead. From security footage it appears you were the last person to see him alive, around 8 p.m. What can you tell me?"

She looked right through Murphy, as if he, and his horrible statement, were not there. And she wished he wasn't, she didn't know if she could maintain her composure in front of him. But she tried.

"David is dead? How can that be?" She stood and straightened piles at the opposite end of the table, she needed to touch something real and solid to ground herself. She finally looked up and knew Murphy noticed the tears in her eyes, but she didn't care. "You have a very insensitive way of announcing a death. I hope you don't do this often."

"Pretty much every day."

After living in Baltimore for years, she wasn't surprised to hear it. "Excuse me, I need a minute." She stepped out and went around the corner to the bathroom. She splashed cold water on her face after having a brief but deep cry.

Murphy was looking over the instruments when she returned. She'd resumed her professional, stoic face as she took her seat. "Thank you for your patience. I'm ready to answer your questions." But she wasn't.

She didn't want to explain what happened.

Murphy spoke as he went back to his seat. "I'll go back to the original. What can you tell me about last night?"

"I took bowings to David in the library around 7 p.m., on my way out for the night." A simple statement seemed like the best place to start.

"What's a bowing?" He asked as he lifted his gaze from his notes.

"It's a set of musical instructions for the string instruments. We have our annual winter solstice concert next week."

A delivery was often their official reason for being in one another's office, but it was never the real reason. Not at that hour, on a Monday, anyway. They were lovers, but not in the way most people would understand. She suppressed a smile after that thought. Both single, they didn't need to keep their relationship secret. Although some members of the board might have frowned upon their workplace relationship, they kept it secret for other reasons. Now, she feared, every private moment would be revealed.

Murphy raised an eyebrow. "Does delivering musical instructions take a lot of time? You were with him for over an hour."

"Sometimes we discuss the changes, and nuances. Occasionally, I will pull out a violin and work through his notes. It can take an hour or longer." Especially when the delivery included a vigorous quickie. She bit her cheek to stop the tears after the realization meetings like last night's would never happen again.

Murphy retrieved a packet of tissues from his pocket and passed one to her. "What else happened?"

She waved off the tissue. "I just explained. I played the violin to refine his instructions. We revised parts. That's it."

"I've watched the security footage. You seem like a lovely person, so don't take this the wrong way," he pointed his pen at her. "You left the library less put together than when you entered."

Anna leaned across the table and glared at him. "What are you implying?" She'd never thought about the damn security cameras giving her away.

"I don't much care what happened as long as he was alive the last time you saw him."

"Of course, he was alive. And smiling!"

"So, you know nothing about the marks on his neck and wrists? Like he was tied up."

She always had a talent for showing no emotion, but her face betrayed her now. She knew about the marks—she'd tied him up with freshly oiled gut strings from the double bass. It had been a kinky quickie.

Murphy, with a grin, as if he already knew the answer, pressed her. "Best to spill the details now. To clear up any misunderstanding."

She wanted to slap the arrogant smirk off Murphy's face. Instead, she responded to his condescending statement with a verbal smack. "I think I'll call my lawyer before I answer any more of your questions."

Murphy pushed back from the table and rose from his seat. "You're welcome to do that. Of course, I'll have to bring you down to the Central District in the meantime. Just tell your lawyer to meet you there." He reached for his handcuffs.

She curled her hands into fists. "You are extremely rude and unprofessional. I'll not be going anywhere with you." While she normally enjoyed being handcuffed, she didn't want the entire staff to see her like that. "Those won't be necessary."

He returned to his place at the table. "Go on."

Anna went straight to the truth. "We were lovers. I did bring the papers I mentioned. But I stayed for sex." She expected a reaction from Murphy but he didn't even look up.

"Pretty much what I thought. Does anyone on staff know you were in a relationship, Maestro?" He said Maestro like he was scolding her.

"No. We kept it between us."

Murphy nodded. "I see. Did you often have sex at work?"

She couldn't sit in one spot any longer. "Once a week, maybe less. I'm turned on by the idea of someone catching us, so he indulges me.

Sometimes we go, I guess I should say went, to a hotel or one of our apartments." She pushed away from the table, moved to the piano, and rested her hand on it; her only friend in the room.

Murphy chuckled. "You have sex in the library once a week and you don't think anyone else knows you're an item?"

Anna put a halt to the rapid-fire questions with a question of her own. "Do you need the entire backstory of our relationship? Or just the details from last night?"

Murphy sighed. "Any information is helpful."

"It galls me to share this with you." She paced for a few minutes and then sat on the piano bench. "We'd been colleagues for a long time, I knew him from my years at a previous symphony. I lured him to Baltimore when I was named Music Director." She stopped and pinched the bridge of her nose. "Good Lord, that sounds awful. It was completely professional between us for years. Things changed, I hate to admit this, at a symphony Christmas party a few years ago. So cliché, but true. We'd both had too many champagne cocktails and discovered something we had in common—BDSM."

Anna made direct eye contact with Murphy, but he had no reaction to that revelation. David became her Dominant after that discussion. She savored the relinquishment of power as a submissive in that part of her life. As one of a handful of female conductors in the world, she controlled nearly every decision at the symphony. She even insisted on using the masculine, Maestro, as nearly all of her female colleagues did, in a nod to tradition.

Many looked at David as a quiet, gentle librarian. He was those things, but he was also passionate with the stamina of a man half his age. As her Dominant, he challenged Anna's strength and tolerance for pain, but at the same time, he was sweet and caring. There were always tender moments after a round of kink. It was the perfect balance for her. She loved how he experimented on her with the instruments. She'd never forget the intense orgasm she'd had when vibrations from the brass of his trumpet met her hungry clit.

She continued. "Doms rarely are the ones tied up, but last night David demanded I do it. He said he wanted me to experience some of the process from his point of view. We were naked on his desk and he handed me the double bass strings."

"Wouldn't the strings cut him?"

"These are natural gut, softer and more pliable than steel."

Murphy nodded. "So bruises, but no cuts. Go on."

She stood and paced. "As he instructed, I wrapped the string around each wrist and then bound them together. Then I stepped back from the desk, and he started with some of my favorite dirty talk." She stopped and looked at Murphy as he dutifully scribbled his notes. "This is gratuitous. Is all of this really necessary?"

Murphy glanced at her over his reading glasses. "Yes. The tiniest detail can change the course of an investigation."

Anna returned to the piano bench and resumed. David had a fantasy where Anna walked around a pool bar in a tiny bikini to pick up men. She loved the details he described, she had a secret longing to be viewed as a sex object. As she stood a few feet away and listened to him, she began to ache for his touch, but he wouldn't let her take one step toward him. It made her burn with need. If she took even a half-step, he added another two minutes to the fantasy. It was torture, as if she wore restraints.

Finally, after twelve minutes, he allowed her to move back to him. With his hands tied, he still couldn't touch her. She became frantic, trying to figure a way into his arms. He told her to stand with her back to him, and he slipped his arms over her head. Then he spread her legs with his and slipped his throbbing cock into her.

For a moment, she had a reprieve from frustration, but not from pain. His bound arms around her neck in a chokehold had her breathing quickly. He also drove his cock so deep inside her, it nearly hurt. And yet, she was still dissatisfied because he couldn't play with her tits.

"I climaxed over and over, finally tapping out after twenty minutes or so. I kissed the bruised wrists when I took the strings off him, and he pulled me into his arms. It was such a relief I cried."

Murphy took a few breaths before his next question. "So, you were in love with him?"

She moved back to the table but didn't take her seat. "No, nothing like that. It was a mutually gratifying physical relationship, no other expectations. Those tears were a release. He led me over to his couch for a cuddle which turned into round two."

Murphy interrupted. "Is that when you put something around his neck?"

"I have no idea what you're talking about. I didn't put anything on his neck. Around 8:30 we got dressed, and I left him with bruised wrists, smiling, satisfied."

Murphy didn't move for a few moments. He flipped back in his notes. "Mr. Mendoza had ligature marks on his wrists and his neck. We'll need the ME to confirm, but all seemed to have happened around the same time."

"I can tell you exactly where I left the bass strings after I took them off him. I don't know a thing about his neck."

Murphy stood up. "Look, Ms. Small, truth is I'm having a hard time seeing you as the BDSM type. Especially as a submissive."

She interrupted. "You're a BDSM expert now?"

"You'd be surprised." He took a deep breath, like he might explain. "As I was saying, you appear sincere and honest. We're still gathering evidence and processing the crime scene."

"There was no crime," Anna barked. She'd done nothing wrong, they were two consenting adults. "If I have to walk down Charles Street in handcuffs to gain my innocence, then we better get started now." She thrust her wrists out in front of her.

"No, I'm not going to handcuff you right now. You'd probably enjoy it too much."

Her jaw dropped, then she hissed, "You're vulgar."

"And occasionally crude. However, I'm not the one who had sex at work last night. Just don't leave the city for the next couple of weeks. I'll have the M.E.'s report in a few days. We'll go from there." He left a business card on the table and departed.

Henri rushed in as soon as Murphy left. "What happened?"

"Get the board president on the phone for me. And ask Cherrie to come to my office as soon as I'm done on the phone. Then gather the staff."

Anna's conversation with the board president was honest—to a point. She told him David was dead, she was a suspect because she was the last one to see him, but she didn't give any additional details. She reiterated her innocence and said the symphony would release information shortly.

Cherrie, the PR and marketing director, crafted a statement and a plan. She didn't mince words with Anna.

"I'm sorry, Maestro, but if you're a suspect you need to take a leave of absence until all this is cleared up."

Anna slammed her hands on her desk. "God dammit. This is insane. Who will know I'm a suspect except you, me, and the police? Rehearsals need to continue for the solstice show."

Cherrie shrugged and stepped toward the door. "This is a small city. You know damn well the police suspicions will get leaked to the press. If you don't take a leave, we'll have to suspend you and that will definitely damage your reputation."

Anna met with the musicians and the staff a couple of hours later. She explained David had died in the office the night before. "I was the last person to see him alive. We've decided it's best for me and the symphony if I take a leave until this is cleared up. The show must go on, of course. Frances will step in as conductor for the solstice rehearsals in the meantime."

Henri, in tears, packed Anna's important items after they returned to her office. "How could such a thing happen? Who'd ever believe you were capable of something so gruesome? This isn't right."

"Thank you, Henri. I'm sure David died of unfortunate natural causes, but because it happened here, they need to investigate it as a crime. I need you to be my eyes and ears while I'm gone. I'm sure there's an explanation that will exonerate me."

As Cherrie predicted, the evening news headlined the death–Anna refused to say murder—with the subtle information she was the last to see him alive. By morning, the national news picked up the story. She couldn't leave her building because of the throng of press on the street.

She picked up Murphy's business card and dialed. "I'm hoping you have an update for me."

"Sorry, Maestro, it's only been twenty-four hours. Is there anything else you'd like to share about Monday night?"

Anna filled a kettle while they talked. "Nothing I can think of. Are you sure David didn't get those marks around his neck from auto-erotic self-asphyxiation? He'd had a habit of it when he was a teen, or so he said."

"You're not exactly a reliable source. I'm in enough trouble for not arresting you yesterday. I'm going to wait for the coroner's report before I take any more information from you."

"Hey, you asked me if I had anything else to share, so I shared."

"You're a snarky one and ballsy for a murder suspect."

She put the kettle on the burner and pulled out a teacup. "You'd be ballsy too if you were fighting for your innocence. You know where to find me if you get new information."

Anna couldn't believe this had happened. For years she kept her peccadillos to herself. She did everything right—got into top schools, studied under the world's best conductors, broke through in a male-dominated field to finally land her own symphony—only to lose it all to her desires. David was an excellent Dom, though hardly her first and, honestly, not worth losing everything over.

She stirred milk and sugar into her tea as she remembered how she took this path. Dozens of years earlier, encouraged by her therapist to embrace her truth, Anna tried her first BDSM experience. She needed discretion, even then, as a rising star, so she chose to attend a party at the den of a Dominatrix. Everyone in attendance had been vetted by the hostess, giving Anna some level of reassurance.

Terrified by the apparatus, tools, and accessories in the dungeon, Anna almost didn't stay that night. A musky scent mixed with citrus and pine reminded her of making out at summer camp, which was, ironically, a comfort. She was swayed by another guest to at least stick around and listen to the orientation. Madame Tocador went over every device, its uses, safety precautions, and the amount of pain it inflicted. Some guests, those experienced with the dungeon, showed no reluctance, and as soon as Madame finished, they began their night.

Anna needed a drink. She went to the bar, poured a tequila, and squeezed a lime into it. When she turned back to the room, Madame approached.

"I don't think this is your scene, little pup. Brand new?"

"Yes, ma'am."

"It's Madame, but I'll forgive you this first time for the mistake. Why don't you come with me?"

Anna almost said no, thank you, but there was something about the grace and kindness in the Dominatrix that intrigued Anna. She never expected a Dominant to exude kindness, especially not one dressed in black leather and accessorized with a crop. Anna, despite her fear, followed Madame upstairs as requested.

This second room was softer and didn't reek of week-old sex. Blankets, pillows, and fur rugs accompanied leather floggers, collars, cuffs, and ropes. "Is this more what you expected?" Madame asked.

"Sort of. I hoped for more intimacy for my first time as a submissive, but then I guess I shouldn't have come to a party."

"Are you truly ready to submit?"

She thought she was when she signed up for the party two weeks ago. She thought she was when she bought new clothes a week ago. She thought she was when she showered and prepped earlier tonight. But, minutes from her first experience, she said, "I'm not sure."

"Let's find out." Madame closed the door. "Take off your clothes down to your panties, and then go sit on the couch in the corner, eyes to the floor."

Anna did as told. Relieved she'd chosen her sexiest bra and panties, she folded her clothes and neatly stacked them on a shelf. She took her bra off too, because she wasn't sure if she should leave it on or not. She sat on the couch, put her hands in her lap, and cast her gaze to the bear skin rug at her feet. Footsteps moved about the room until finally, Madame's heels came into view.

"Very good, little pup. From this point on you will abide by every instruction. Say yes if you consent."

Anna said, "Yes, Madame."

She tied a blindfold over Anna's eyes, then lifted her chin and kissed her gently followed by a quick, sharp bite on her lower lip. Next, a supple piece of leather bound her hands together and a collar encircled her neck.

"I'm clipping a leash on you, then you'll stand and follow where I lead."

Anna heard the click and stood. She felt a tug and moved in that direction until told to stop. The leash was removed. "Now, raise your arms over your head." Madame tugged Anna's arms a little higher forcing her to stand on tiptoes, and then suspended Anna's arms from, what she could best surmise, a metal chain.

Lips were on her again. "You are stunning in this pose."

Anna wasn't sure if she should respond but a thank you seemed appropriate. "Thank you, Madame."

"My pleasure, little pup."

The next kiss caused a warm tingle between Anna's legs which turned into a gush when clamps were placed on her nipples.

A finger slid into her panties. "Little pup is enjoying the pain."

Euphoric from this first experience, combined with the agony of realizing her painful desires, brought on tears. They escaped the blindfold and gave her away. Madame rewarded her with an orgasm and several smacks with the paddle, then she lowered Anna back to her feet.

"I hope little pup bruises easily so you'll see these marks tomorrow and relive your first submissive orgasm." Madame took off the clamps and the blindfold. She grabbed Anna's hand and guided her back to the couch. "What I do next, I usually have one of my minions do as a service. However, I think it's more appropriate tonight that I take care of this myself." Madame instructed Anna to lie on the couch, covered her with blankets, and cuddled her for a few minutes.

Surprised by this tender moment, Anna wept. "I'm sorry Madame," she said. "I don't cry often. Tonight is the most I've cried in years."

"Never apologize for your tears. Your vulnerability is beautiful." Madame kissed Anna again. "That's enough for tonight, even though brief. Get dressed and go home. I'll be in touch for more lessons."

Anna's phone rang and brought her out of her rumination. She put her tea cup in the sink before she answered.

It was Henri. He'd gone home early, distraught from the events. "I can't be in that place right now," he explained. "The staff is being completely disloyal. The rumors about you are ugly."

"What are they saying?" She wanted to know if her relationship with David had been revealed.

"Such terrible things, Maestro. If I'd known this was going to happen, I'd have taken care of it sooner."

She paced the hallway in her apartment passing the pile of holiday decoration she'd yet to put up. Not likely it would happen now. "Taken care of what?" What did Henri know?

"Doing something about your relationship with that cruel misogynist."

She slumped onto the floor, next to a large Christmas wreath her mother made years ago. Maybe Murphy was right and many on staff knew. "What are you talking about?"

"I know what David has been doing to you. It's not my business, but you shouldn't be treated that way." The shrill in his voice penetrated her eardrum.

She let out a long sigh. "Henri, what did you do?"

"I gave him a stern talking to. He didn't even acknowledge me. Can you believe it?"

"Yes! Because it was none of your business. He did nothing wrong. Neither of us did." Anna hauled herself off the floor and moved to her piano, her refuge, and lifted the lid. "Is that all you did, talk to him?"

"A very stern talk. Nearly yelling."

"When?"

"Monday night. After you left."

She ran her fingers over the piano keys. The ordered ebony and ivory was the only thing that made sense to her. "Why didn't the detective see you on the security footage?"

"I don't know. I wasn't sneaky about it."

Perhaps Murphy stopped watching the security footage after he saw Anna go in and out of the library? That didn't sound as thorough as Little-Staten suggested. Could Henri have killed David? Her shoulders drooped.

"Have you been interviewed by Murphy yet?"

He sniffled. "This morning. Maestro, I promise, I protected you."

Anna slammed the keyboard lid. "I'll say again, you have no idea what our relationship was. Stay home until you hear from me. And stop crying."

She ended the call with Henri and dialed Murphy.

He didn't bother with hello. "You need to stop calling me, it's inappropriate."

"My innocence is inappropriate? Tough shit. You gave me your card twice, if you don't want people to call, then stop handing it out."

"Still snarky. Still no coroner's report, either."

Anna looked at the grandfather clock across the living room. "That's not why I'm calling. Does Henri's information exonerate me?" Nearly noon, she went to her liquor cabinet and poured herself a finger of scotch.

"What information?"

She tried to sip the scotch but knew a second one would be forthcoming. She truly hated when others played coy. "Henri said you interviewed him this morning. He didn't mention he'd been in the library after I'd left?"

"I can't divulge what I've discovered in other interviews."

"Then why did you ask 'what information'?"

"Anna…"

"Maestro!" Her outburst surprised her. She'd never been so adamant about the use of her title but then she'd never been a suspect for murder either.

Murphy apologized. "Maestro, if you have some new information, you're welcome to share it with me. Why don't we meet?"

"I can't leave the building. It's reporter mania downstairs."

He agreed to come to her place around three.

After a shower, she put on one of her professional suits, so as not to appear disheveled two days in a row. She even decided to wear purple suede pumps to match her blouse. Murphy knocked at half-past three, holding two coffees, and wearing jeans and a polo shirt. A better look for him.

"Detective Murphy, you look relaxed today."

"These are my off-duty duds, Maestro."

Anna led him to the kitchen where she served coffee cake. "I'm sorry about all of this Maestro stuff. I mean, it is my honorific, but I'm not usually such an ass about it. As you can imagine, I've not been myself since yesterday. Please, call me Anna."

He waved off the slice of coffee cake. "I wouldn't dare, Maestro. Why don't you tell me this new information from Henri?"

She shared the details of her conversation with Henri between stabs at her piece of cake. She couldn't eat. "He said he went into the library after I left. So why am I the main suspect?"

"I'll double check the security footage. I only watched the segment Little-Staten gave me."

"You've ruined my life with these accusations and you didn't even watch the entire video from the whole night?"

His left leg started to bounce up and down. "It didn't seem necessary. I'll correct that immediately." He stood and pulled out his phone. "I'll let myself out."

Anna cleaned the kitchen, then opened her laptop. She'd avoided almost all communication since Monday afternoon but knew her sister would be worried so an email seemed in order. Anna didn't want to call. She didn't think she could speak the words aloud, not to Christine. For the first time ever, Anna was relieved her parents had passed away. Explaining to Christine would be difficult enough. Explaining it to their parents would've been impossible.

Anna's personal email was filled with notes of support. For the first time in a couple of days, she smiled as she read messages from colleagues, old friends, former students, and musicians she'd performed with all over the world. She didn't respond, she didn't have the words at the moment to properly express her gratitude, and she needed to use what little she had in her emotional vocabulary to contact her sister.

After nearly two hours of reading emails and crafting a message to Christine, Anna closed her computer and checked her phone. Nothing new from Murphy. She took the phone and went to her bedroom to lie down. She changed out of her suit and put on her coziest sweatshirt and leggings—the go-to when she needed a hug and no one was around to give her one. Before she closed her eyes or tried to, she double checked the ringer on her phone was turned all the way up.

She tried a few meditations to quiet her mind, she needed the sleep, she'd had little the night before, but it was futile. Luckily, the phone rang so she gave up the battle for the moment. It was Murphy.

"I can barely stand to be with myself much longer. I hope you have some news."

Murphy cleared his throat. "I do and I also have an apology. I'm sorry my investigation wasn't up to par. There was more on the security footage and now I'm following up some other leads."

Anna threw off her blanket and sat up. "That sounds positive. What does it mean for me?"

"Honestly," Murphy sighed, "I'm not sure yet. I'll know more by this time tomorrow."

"Will I be able to take my rightful spot at the solstice concert next week?" It was the first positive thought Anna had since Monday night.

"I can't make any promises."

"I'm taking that as a yes."

Anna padded to the kitchen after hanging up with Murphy. She heated soup and ate about half, not much but at least she had a bit of appetite. Exhaustion caught up with her. As she walked back to her bedroom, she stopped to hang her mother's Christmas wreath. She climbed back into bed and was asleep in minutes.

Early Thursday afternoon, Murphy called from Anna's lobby. He didn't want to give her the news over the phone so hoped it was okay to stop by on short notice. She invited him up.

This time they sat in the living room. She was still in her cozy sweatshirt but had put on jeans before he knocked. She'd lit a blueberry candle earlier and the whole apartment smelled like muffins. She didn't know what he would tell her but good news or bad, the aroma of baked goods made it easier for her to hear.

Murphy chose to stand. "We have Henri and Little-Staten in custody. It's just a matter of time before they roll over on one another. I wanted you to hear it from me before the press or the people in your office find out."

Anna sat on the arm of her sofa. "One of them murdered David?"

"No, but they tried." Murphy explained what he knew about their scheme. Little-Staten had shared stories with Henri about Anna's comings and goings to the library. They pieced together months of surveillance video with the rumors about Anna and David. "Instead of confronting you, Little-Staten convinced Henri to confront David to save your reputation. He's doggedly loyal to you."

"To a fault. Henri tried to strangle David? He can barely open a package of pencils. I'm shocked he had the strength for something so gruesome."

"Your instincts are excellent. Henri didn't try to strangle David but he did bring a rope and coerced David to do it himself. Apparently, there were threats made, some of that isn't clear yet."

Anna stood and walked to her bar. "I need a drink. This is my fault. David's dead, Henri is a murderer, and for what? So I could get sexual satisfaction. I deserve to be punished, not Henri."

"You certainly do deserve punishment." Murphy winked. "Don't wallow in your guilt too quickly. Henri and Little-Staten are only charged with obstructing an investigation and other minor felonies, so far. Henri didn't murder David. The coroner called this morning, David's cause of death was an aneurysm around 10 p.m. He was likely alone but we're trying to find out why he hadn't left the building after the confrontation with Henri."

Anna swallowed the lump in her throat. "How awful. And all by himself."

"Those things come on fast," Murphy explained. "Could've been the stress of the evening's events. He likely never knew what hit him." He handed her a napkin for her tears even though she tried to fight them.

She turned and cocked an eyebrow at him. "Is that some kind of warped BDSM joke?"

Murphy moved toward her front door. "Never. Maestro, that is something I take very seriously. You mentioned yesterday you have two of my cards. Keep one nearby. When you're done grieving, give me a call." He winked again and left.

Piano Tuning
Anna V. Nelson

I sat at the back of the hall as the symphony rehearsed for the live performance. The conductor had included Tchaikovsky's No. 1 in B-flat major. He said he wanted something comfortingly familiar to make the audience feel the lockdown hadn't occurred, that it was just yesterday listeners had enjoyed a live performance. My husband Oscar was thrilled he'd been hired as the pianist although he told me he would have preferred a more challenging piece for his considerable talents. All the musicians were excited about the upcoming performance and worked hard at each rehearsal to make it their best work.

I should have been happy for them, but instead, I was anxious. Oscar had grown increasingly morose over the pandemic year—many of us were down—but his sadness worked its way into our sex life. The bedroom had been the last place any issues between us arose. Oscar had special needs when it came to lovemaking. I had accommodated him by working around his issues, which were not the usual fetishes or anomalies in sex play. You see, Oscar was a strangler. He liked to put his hands around my throat at the moment of my orgasm, believing it would enhance my experience. Or so he said. I suspected it was more for him than for me. When we tried it, his yelling and the violent shuddering of his body revealed his orgasms were multiplied a thousand-fold when he cut off my air supply. I hated it. I was certain he would succeed in killing me. A struggle to breathe was not my idea of coming hard. It was more like dying hard. It made me feel as if the grave reached out to take me—sheer terror.

"Oscar," I'd told him, "You know I love you dearly, but this has got to stop. We need another way to express our lust for each another."

"You find one, dear Abbie, one that makes me quiver and thrash like a madman, and I'll agree to it."

He thought I wouldn't come up with anything, but I did and quickly. He was thrilled and so was I. Both our orgasms were magnificent. Clever me.

I left off my musings about sex and leaned forward in my seat at the back of the rehearsal hall to get a better look at the members of the orchestra. My, oh, my. They'd taken on a new cello player, and what a player she was. Her long brown hair tumbled around her shoulders. She seemed to envelop the instrument as if it were a lover she was possessing. This woman thrust her pelvis into the cello as if it were her sex partner. The exaggerated movements of her body seemed to draw attention away from the music and direct it to her playing. Her head dipped and shifted from side to side while her face registered a look of extreme emotion, almost as if she were about to come. I held my breath and waited for her to cry out in ecstasy. Instead, as the piece came to an end, her eyes rolled back in her head. She moved the bow off the strings and arched her back, pushing her breasts forward. She let forth a short laugh, and then provocatively tossed her hair back. Not only was I aware of her impassioned playing, but the hush in the hall told me she held members of the orchestra spellbound.

Her behavior appeared to create more fury than sexual appetite in many of the female players. One could almost hear the clucks and tsks from them. Several curled their lips in scorn. The men's reactions were another matter. A few licked their lips while others moved around in their chairs as if their pants were suddenly too tight. Most upsetting was my Oscar's reaction. From his position at the piano, he sat as stiff as a corpse, then raised his gaze and looked toward me. I knew he couldn't see me in the back of the theater, but he knew I was there. He tilted his head and his gaze bored into me. I read his message. "Beware," it said. I knew things would never be the same between us.

* * *

"So, I noticed you have a new cello player," I said as Oscar and I relaxed in our apartment later that night.

He laughed. "You and every musician there noticed."

"What's her name?"

"Stella." Oscar gulped down the last of the brandy in his snifter and held out his hand to me. "Let's go to bed, my dear."

In our softly lit bedroom, Oscar stood at the foot of our bed and nodded to me. I dropped to my knees and began to remove his clothes. As I stripped his shorts from him, it was clear he was aroused and ready. His long, hard penis seemed to quiver in anticipation.

I pointed to the bed, and he sank onto it, his eyes dark with lust. He liked when I took command. I grabbed his hands, then his feet, and bound him to the four-poster bed with the expensive silk scarves I purchased for our shared hunger. He seemed always to enjoy the bondage ritual I recommended as the way to keep his hands from my throat. As he watched, I removed my dress, then my bra and panties. As usual at this point in our lovemaking, his penis signaled an increased ache for me as it grew larger and seemed to lengthen. I crawled onto the bed and ran my tongue over it. I loved it. I loved him, and the feeling of him against my lips and mouth made me shiver with desire. He groaned as he watched me sweep my tongue up and down the shaft. I reached into the bed table drawer and took out a condom, unwrapped it, and slid it onto him. I straddled him and slipped him back and forth along my lips, then inserted his tip into my vagina to begin the in and out, in and out, and deeper and deeper repetition, the favorite tease of ours that always made both of us throb and ache with the need for more. But not this time. He softened.

"Too much brandy, I guess." He was lying. It was the remembrance of seeing Stella publicly seduce her instrument earlier this evening that interfered with his performance.

"Untie me." He chuckled once freed. He removed the condom, got up, and went into the bathroom. I heard the shower. He emerged in a few minutes with a towel wrapped around his hips. "I took a short one tonight. There's lots of hot water left. I'm so sorry, Abbie, but there's always tomorrow. Right now, I'm for bed." He gave me a kiss on the cheek, flicked my nipple with his finger, and slid under the sheets. He began to breathe slower as sleep overtook him. His lips curved in a smile, one I wasn't responsible for putting there.

I got up and went into the bathroom and discovered he did what he always did—threw the used condom into the trash. Why couldn't he flush it? I picked it out of the waste can and tossed it into the toilet, gave a flush, and decided against a shower. Instead, I went into the kitchen for a cup of tea. I added a shot of bourbon, hoping the alcohol would relax me. It didn't. I knew what Oscar and I once had was gone.

I didn't usually go to rehearsals, only the one the night before the performance, and only if Oscar played. My presence there earlier tonight was because the orchestra hadn't played together for so long. I longed to see Oscar's beautiful fingers dance across the keys. To see him at the keyboard was almost like foreplay for me. Those hands were what attracted me to him. I regretted I'd been forced to tie them to be certain they didn't accidentally wrap around my throat. I knew he'd never intentionally strangle me to death, but I couldn't risk a mistake. Often, while I moved up and down on him and he thrust himself into me, I'd bent over and licked his fingers. The feeling of my soft wetness wrapped around him along with my tongue on his fingertips brought him to a climax so powerful he seemed to lose consciousness. As for me, seeing him so moved by my love making was sublime.

I feared his fascination with Stella's passionate engagement with her instrument meant Oscar and I would never experience each other in quite the same way. His performance in our bed tonight was a sign of the future. Although Oscar had never taken another lover since we had met and married over a decade ago, from this night on, I knew he would no longer find our passion quite as satisfying as before. He would, of course, put his strong slender fingers around her long, exquisite neck, and quite by accident, he would squeeze the life out of her. Maybe not today or tomorrow, but eventually. He wouldn't be able to help himself.

I couldn't go to her and tell her that her life was in danger. She wasn't likely to believe me, the wife of the man I knew she would seduce as passionately as she had her instrument.

* * *

The following night at the cocktail party, after the performance, I circulated among the musicians and eavesdropped on conversations. Stella seemed to be a favorite topic. As everyone suspected, Stella was not only lustful with her instrument; it seemed she meant to extend the same ardent attention toward as many men as she could. Rumors said she was working her way through the horn section. From bassoonist Howard Loft's satisfied smile each time he looked at her to both male clarinet players who hovered so close around her, the talk had to be true. Worries swirled in my head. When would she get to Oscar? How much time did I have? Where would they go to enjoy each other? Stella had a roommate, so her place was out. Oscar couldn't bring her back to our place. My only defense was vigilance.

"You're lucky you have Oscar, Abbie. He adores you. Some of the men won't be able to resist her." Rose Martin played clarinet and must have read my expression. She and I were friends, not close enough for me to confide anything about Oscar and our relationship, but we skyped now and then during lockdown and had resumed having weekly lunches together.

"I guess that's why most of the female musicians didn't bring their husbands, partners, or a date with them tonight." I looked around the room and noticed Stella had nabbed one of the male members of the orchestra volunteer committee.

"Oh, oh. Look at that. Poor Jethro has been cornered by Stella," said Nancy Hardy, another member of the committee. "Should I go save him?"

"Does he look like he wants to be rescued?" I asked. My tone was biting.

"I'm not certain he knows he's in danger," said Rose. We all laughed, me perhaps not as sincerely as the others when I realized there was only one place for Oscar and Stella to meet: the theatre, after rehearsals when everyone had gone.

* * *

Since Oscar was scheduled to play with the orchestra the coming month also, I took up hiding in the darkened back of the hall after each rehearsal. I watched until everyone left the theater. Oscar often grabbed a ride home with one of the French horn players or caught a taxi, leaving our car with me. I was finishing my advanced degree in Greek history and did research at the city library until it closed. The car was my only way home unless I took a late bus. Oscar felt that wasn't safe.

For over a week, nothing happened between Stella and Oscar. In fact, Oscar and I returned to our sex ritual. Oscar seemed as eager as ever. I loved riding him to a climax, mine following right behind. After he got up and tossed the condom, he returned to bed to snuggle with me. Sometimes we read to each other or listened to music and sipped coffee and brandy. Our lives seemed perfect. Still, I had a feeling not all was right between us.

My spying paid off. One night after rehearsal, I saw Stella whisper to him. His tongue moved across his lips, then he bent and spoke into her ear. His fingers caressed the side of her cheek, then trailed over her chin onto her long, slender neck. I could almost see the pulse in her throat quicken at his touch. My own heart began to race. I hated this woman, but sooner or later, Oscar would lose himself in his lust, apply too much pressure, and kill her. I had to watch him and stop him. I continued my vigil, shaking with tension because I knew what was to come. When everyone left the theatre that night, except for Stella and Oscar, he sat at the piano, ran his fingers over the keyboard, and then closed it. He spun to face away from the instrument. The sound was so good in the hall I heard him say, "Take off your clothes so I can see you."

Stella moved out of the shadows, a naked figure, white, long-legged, large-breasted. She flipped her hair to one side, just as she had when she played. She moved her body sinuously as she strode on stiletto heels to the piano bench. Oscar leaned back with his arms across the keyboard.

Stella bent and unzipped him, reached into his pants, and drew out his erect penis.

"A lovely thing," she said.

Oscar smirked. "Just the right size for a big girl like you. Come. Sit."

Oscar moved his torso off the keyboard and sat upright on the bench. Stella straddled him. He moved his hands to her throat, then hesitated. "We need this." He held up a condom and started to open the package.

"Don't bother." She slipped off him and buried her head in his lap.

Stella took only a few minutes before Oscar heaved and groaned.

"You've got quite a mouth on you, more like a gal who plays a wind instrument rather than someone who fiddles with strings."

Stella licked her lips. "When you're ready, I can show you some finger work, but now, you do me."

And he did. I watched. Anger grew inside me.

These trysts went on for several weeks. Why no intercourse for Stella? Why always oral sex? I watched them and felt the need rise inside him. He sometimes sat on our living room couch in the evenings curling and uncurling his fingers, then he would get up, grab my hand, and take me into the bedroom. We enacted our ritual, but I knew he was never really satisfied with me. I realized he felt a sense of incompleteness with Stella, too. He wanted more. I knew what it was. Their trysts were repeated as they had begun. My concern grew, as did my fury.

Two nights before the final rehearsal for the May performance, Oscar and I had intercourse. It felt like the days before Stella. He was harder, harder than I ever remembered. He moaned and hissed like a man so far gone in lust that when he came, I thought the condom would blow apart. Had Stella taken another lover? He hadn't been with her for several nights.

I untied him and sank beside him. Perhaps he and Stella had parted ways.

He jumped out of bed and strode into the bathroom. I heard the toilet flush and he returned.

"I love you, you know." I twisted my body into his.

"You exhausted me tonight." The words were what a woman wanted to hear from a man she'd just made love to, but his tone was accusatory, almost as if he implied I had ruined him somehow.

I rose on one elbow to look at him, but his eyes were closed. His breath came deep and regular. I had exhausted him. He had fallen asleep.

I got out of bed to go to the bathroom. There it was. The condom in the waste basket. I bent to retrieve it, but instead, went into the kitchen and grabbed a plastic baggie. Returning to the bathroom, I grabbed my tweezers and dropped the used condom into the baggie which I slipped into my robe pocket. I looked at my image in the bathroom mirror. I did not look like a woman sated from sex. I looked like a deceived wife filled with rage.

"I love you, too, you know," he said as I slipped back into bed.

"Yes." I turned on my side and pretended to sleep.

* * *

I went to the library the next afternoon and worked until it was time for the rehearsal. When I rushed to my car so I wouldn't miss the final rehearsal, a late spring snow, wet and heavy, was falling. The forecast had been for a few inches, but it looked as if this was going to be more.

I cleaned off the car and headed into traffic, aiming for the rehearsal hall. The car slid from one side to the other on the slippery streets, and I had to slow down. I told myself there was no need to hurry. Stella wasn't important to Oscar. I was. He had given her up. They hadn't met for days, almost a week. Last night with Oscar marked a new beginning in our desire for each other. Oscar knew what I could do for him… what I would do for him.

When I got to the hall, it appeared most of the musicians had gone. I ran inside and took up my position in the back. Oscar said good night to several of the orchestra members and stood alone on the stage. He ran his fingers across the keyboard, and played part of Beethoven's No.

5, the selection for tomorrow night. Stella was nowhere in sight. I wanted to call out to him and tell him I was here to give him a ride home, but I hesitated. He removed all his clothes and sat on the piano bench, taking up his usual position, leaning back onto the closed keyboard, casual, relaxed except his penis was enlarged and erect and ready for…

I heard a rustle and Stella appeared out of the dark, walking toward him, naked as he was.

He reached out to her, and she came to him. She nodded. He reached out for the condom packet on the closed keyboard. He held it out to her, and she slipped it on him, then mounted him. Nothing oral this time, not even a kiss. He reached for her breasts and caressed them with his hands, then began a teasing, flicking of her nipples. She groaned and moved up and down faster and faster. He tipped his head back and howled, then grabbed her throat and squeezed. I froze in place, my hands over my mouth, horrified with what I knew could happen but wanted to believe never would. I should have called out, but I didn't. Her body went limp.

He stood and stared toward where I had been hiding.

"Were you too late tonight or did you enjoy the event so much you got lost in it?" He smiled. "Did you think I'd never get my way with her?" He grabbed his clothes, put them on, and exited.

How did he know I watched him? Was I to blame for not stopping him? But what could I have done? Was I as much to blame for Stella's death as he was? I thought about my guilt for only a moment, then I did what was necessary.

I don't know where he dumped the condom they'd used, perhaps into the river or a trash barrel streets away. He went home. I didn't. Instead, I called my sister and told her I didn't want to drive all the way to the apartment in the bad weather so could I please spend the night with her? She lived only a few blocks from the library.

The janitor found Stella's body the next morning. I made the job easier for the police . Oscar's DNA was in the condom I'd discarded in the waste can in the men's lavatory off-stage. The authorities made the arrest the next evening, right before Oscar left for the performance, just as I returned to the apartment from my work in the library.

"Where have you been?" he asked me. His face was red and distorted with fury.

"I stayed with my sister last night, went right from there to the library this morning. I rushed home now to change for the program. Officers, what's going on?"

"We're arresting your husband for the murder of Stella Miller, one of his colleagues."

"Oscar? He wouldn't do such a thing."

Oscar struggled as they cuffed him. "Tell them we were together last night."

"Oscar, you know that's not true. I stayed with my sister because of the treacherous streets. I called and left a message on your cell. Didn't you check it?"

Of course, he didn't. He hadn't noticed my absence or cared about it. The intensity of his orgasm with Stella would have smoldered through the night. Behind the fear and anger, his passionate triumph still burned in his eyes. Was it the best orgasm of his life?

It was probably his last.

* * *

I was the aggrieved wife, cheated on by a husband who then killed his lover. I refused to visit him in jail. My pain was too great to attend his trial—his truly short trial—which ended in a guilty verdict. I burned the silk scarves. I wanted no memories of how clever I thought I was to find another way to satisfy a man whose desperate desire to strangle finally killed a woman. It could have been me. And, no. I don't feel responsible for her death. Certainly, it's sad to lose such musical talent. All the women associated with the orchestra feel that way. What they don't admit, and I share this with them is, we are relieved she is no longer here. I'll bet the men don't agree.

Fools.

The Tail
Chandler Christie

"Nice place you got here."

The curl of Nico Benedetto's lip and the lift of his eyebrow said he didn't mean it. I sized him up while I moved a stack of manila folders from my guest chair to my desk. Thinning slicked-back hair dyed to match his heavy black eyebrows. Deep-set eyes. Five-nine or ten in freshly polished wingtips, one-eighty in a bulging charcoal pin-striped suit. Too many carbs and not enough exercise for a guy pushing fifty.

That figured. Nico's Pizzeria had mushroomed in the six years since he opened it in North Beach: spun off Trattoria Nico, then a deli, then a gelateria. I couldn't argue with his prize-winning tomato sauce, but Nico Benedetto was pitching to the tourists, not the locals. Too pricey for a private eye doing business out of a third-floor walk-up that dated back to the 1906 earthquake.

"Where's your secretary?" he asked me as we shook hands. "What's her name, Velma?"

"Unusually heavy call volume. Velma's busy assisting other customers."

"Ha ha. Which one are you? Spade or Archer?"

"Spade." I nodded at the empty wooden chair. "What can I do for you, Mr. Benedetto?

He lingered by the window, frowning at the twilight in Washington Square Park. "You got the same sax player down there who panhandles outside my Trattoria."

"No panhandling here. The sidewalk cafe pays him. Their customers like the music."

Nico took a seat, arms folded. "So, this is confidential, right? Like a lawyer?"

"Anything we discuss is protected by my discretion. It's not privileged. I don't take on clients who play chicken with the law. So far, twelve years, no complaints."

"Yeah. That's what I heard." He faced me. "I want you to tail my wife."

"I don't take divorce cases, either."

"No divorce. 'Till death do us part.' We swore, both of us. Right over there," he pointed out the window. "Married at Saints Peter and Paul. Our kids were baptized. We'll be buried there. Joelle and me, together."

"Okay. What are you after, then, if you don't—?"

"I want you to find out where she goes on Thursday nights."

"Why?"

"None of your goddam business."

I stood up. "Nice meeting you, Mr. Benedetto."

"Hold on. Hold on." Nico shook his head so hard that two strands of hair flicked back and forth across his forehead like windshield wipers. "Can we not make a big thing out of this? Keep it simple."

Most of my clients start with that hope. I haven't found it does any good to tell them it's a long shot. Anyhow, Nico Benedetto wouldn't have heard me. In his mind, the interview phase was over. He was committed. Now it was time to agree on what the job entailed.

He was asking if I knew how he and Joelle met. I gave him points for jumping right in without asking what it would cost him.

No, I said, I'd missed his Columbus Day interview on KPIX. And his heart-warming success story in the Chronicle.

"I dated her older sister in high school. Tammy. Down the Peninsula. Her whole family was musical, and me and Tammy were in the San Giovanni High School orchestra. I'd go over for Sunday dinner and we'd all play together. Me on trumpet, Tammy on violin, their brother Roy on double bass, and Joelle banging away on a woodblock and triangle. Six-year-old percussionist! We lost touch after my family moved up here. I went to restaurant school in Italy and lived with my

Nonna for a coupla years. Tammy married a techie, Roy died in a car accident, left Joelle his bass. Long story short, I went back for the funeral, and damn! The kid's grown up. I said, that's the girl I'm gonna marry."

"Just like that?"

"Well," his grin twitched. "It took a while. She wanted me to join her jazz combo, but I'd already lined up backers for the pizza joint, with a good shot at the Trattoria, so..." He shrugged.

"She didn't mind?"

"She understood. These kind of guys, no messing around. Anyhow, Joelle's great. Principal cello for the Pacific Heights Chamber Orchestra."

"What's the issue about Thursday nights?"

Nico crossed his legs and interlaced his fingers around his knee. "Rehearsal. Only time they can use the church hall. She says. Sometimes they go till two or three a.m." His knuckles cracked. "That's bullshit. I ran into my pal Danny, second violin. He said they gotta be out by ten."

"You asked your wife? What'd she say?"

"First, Danny's wrong. Then, half wrong. They have to leave the church, but if they're not done, some of them go over to Jocelyn's and play in her garage."

I waited. I wasn't sure why that was also bullshit, but I figured Nico would tell me.

"You're not a musician."

"No," I said.

"Trust me. You don't pack a chamber orchestra into an SUV and go finish rehearsal in somebody's garage."

"So, what's she up to?" I leaned back. "Girls' night out? Have a drink with her pals?"

"Do I look stupid? Not till three a.m."

"You think she's seeing somebody?"

"You tell me, Spade." He reached toward the bulge inside his jacket. My hand went to the drawer where I keep my Beretta. "If you asked me a month ago I'd've said, no fucking way." Nico pushed an iPhone across the desk. I exhaled and took it. "Gorgeous woman, right? Older husband. I mean, Jesus, I'm on fucking heart meds! Sure. My wife gets hit on all the time. But I'm not stupid and she isn't either. I give her everything she wants. Big allowance. Fantastic sex, always. Two beautiful kids. She'd have to be a moron to throw that away."

"Okay," I said. "What I'm hearing is this. You want everything to stay like it is. Your family, your business, all great. Whatever your wife is up to, you won't divorce her. Why hire me to rock the boat?"

Nico Benedetto slid his phone back into his pocket. "I worked hard to get where I am. Blood and sweat, not walking around blindfolded. I don't want you to rock the boat. Just keep a look out. Watch for torpedoes."

His hand was still inside his jacket. I thought he looked like Napoleon and that probably wasn't an accident.

I said, "I'll check with my partner, Mr. Archer. Assuming we don't have a schedule conflict, Velma will send you an estimate and a contract."

"When?"

"Tomorrow. Monday at the latest."

"This is Thursday! You oughta start tonight."

I smiled at him. "The last time I ate at your Trattoria, I waited four days for a reservation, twenty minutes for a table, and half an hour for dinner. I'll do my best, Mr. Benedetto. You'll hear from us soon. Monday at the latest."

He grimaced and walked out without a goodbye. I went to the window. His shoulders were still hunched as he left the building and crossed the street to the park.

The saxophonist on the corner shaded his eyes, squinting up past the streetlight. I waved and gave him a thumbs-up. He bowed to the diners under their sidewalk umbrellas, capped his mouthpiece, slung his sax over his shoulder, and sauntered after Nico Benedetto.

My cue to hand this case off to Velma. I couldn't do that until showtime, so I went home, changed out of my detective slacks and jacket into black jeans, and watched the evening news.

Archer and I met up an hour later at Sarafina's, the cafe downstairs from our office. The owner and chef is also our landlady, which gives us a mutual interest in shoring up her income. Sarafina serves the best mushroom, onion, and pepperoni pizza in San Francisco, plus a bottle of chianti, for less than Nico's Pizzeria charges for garlic bread.

"How's Velma?" Archer asked me.

"Good. Ready to roll."

"She better be," he grinned. "She started this."

"He started this," I said. "Velma's the bait."

"And the hook."

"You dropped off your sax at the club?"

"Yeah." Archer rubbed his chin. "And my beard. Damn, that itches! Did the cornstarch all come out of my hair?"

"Looks like it. Check with your girlfriend."

He laughed. "Roger that. You got your pocket pal?"

I patted my Beretta in its hip holster. "Roger that."

He dumped out the hatful of bills and change Sarafina's customers had donated for their musical entertainment and took off. That was our tip. I paid the check. With luck, I'd recoup it from the job we'd just set in motion.

On the other side of the park, I joined the late-night flow of thrill-seekers migrating from restaurants to bars. The dark sky was bright with lights of every size and color, humming with car and motorcycle engines, heavy with smells of garlic and olive oil, booze and exhaust fumes, and cologne-drenched tourists, male and female and everything in between. I made a phone call, then drifted with the crowd down Columbus Avenue. There was a line on the sidewalk outside Bingo's Lounge, but one of the bouncers waved me through.

"Welcome, welcome, my friends!" I dodged the host steering incoming guests to seats around the dance floor. My spot was up front at the bar. Velma had saved me the last stool, at the end of the curved row, next to the fire exit. I'd have a clear view of the floor, the cocktail tables, and the raised boxes behind them, but not the band. No problem; that was Archer's part of the job. Mine was Bingo's famous mermaid.

I'd seen this show before and it got me every time. Behind the center of the bar, where normally you'd find a large mirror reflecting shelves of booze bottles, Bingo's had a tank. It looked like a squared-off TV screen: a glowing aquamarine box about two feet tall, two feet wide, and two inches deep. You'd glance at it from the bar, the rocks on the bottom, red and yellow coral fans wafting in the water, and you'd look for fish. There were no fish. Every half hour the water would bubble. The dance floor lights would dim. A hush would spread from the bar to the cocktail tables. And through the bubbles, the mermaid would appear.

Some people murmured, some people wisecracked. It's plastic. No, I swear, it's real. How can it be real? She's the size of a Barbie doll. It's a magic trick. It's a hologram. A video streamed from a hidden projector. Omigod, look! It is real! She sees us! She's waving! It's a real live mermaid!

It was Velma.

She'd given Archer and me a backstage tour. Yes, the mermaid was real; yes, it was a magic trick. An underwater performance by a buff chick wearing a blonde plastic wig with a breathing tube, starfish over her nipples, and a waterproof fish tail. It had to be waterproof because the custom-fitted suit cost a fortune, so Bingo's only had one. Twenty minutes between shows wasn't enough time to dry it out. If it got wet inside there was absolutely no way to put it back on.

Velma had been the Bingo's mermaid for four years before she applied to Spade and Archer for a day job. Aside from the benefits and career path, she liked swimming way more than office work. She performed in a full-size heated tank in the basement with mirrors that reflected up through the ceiling to the miniature tank behind the bar. Qualifications? High-school breast-stroke champion (stretching to show off her assets). Publicity? Forget about it. No filming, no interviews. Why? Did Bingo's make her sign a nondisclosure agreement? No, or she wouldn't be talking to us. She just couldn't take the crap questions: Aren't you scared you'll drown? I try not to think about it, thanks very much. How do you go to the bathroom? Same holes as you, dimwit. Have you ever had sex as a mermaid? Fuck off.

I surveyed the scene from my barstool. The little tank was empty, but the club was packed. Archer claimed this was Bingo's real magic trick: passers-by who might toss him a quarter in the park would stand in line six hours later and pay a big fat cover charge to hear him play the same tunes. He figured it must be the decor. Aside from Velma's aquatic sideshow, the club's theme was Jazz Age: black walls, black-and-silver carpets, chrome railings, and thin gold and white lines on the tablecloths and lampshades. Also, a lot of triangles. I thought of six-year-old Joelle, the aspiring percussionist. Who switched to strings when she grew up. Who set aside her dead brother's bass to marry Nico Benedetto.

The tank was bubbling. Enough second-hand nostalgia. Show time!

My instructions were to find my way downstairs and stand behind the folding screen in the small room that held the tank. Velma had taped an X on the concrete floor. If I wanted to shoot her performance, I'd have to exactly match the mirror set-up that shrank and beamed it up to the bar. And don't make a sound! This was her act, okay? Bingo's crew chief had taken care of video and audio. She'd prepped our target and didn't expect any trouble. Still, you never know. I and my phone and my Beretta were welcome back-ups.

We didn't speak. Just as well. Real-life Velma in a baggy sweatshirt and tights, crimson lipstick, and a Goth crewcut added flair to the office of Spade and Archer. A ten-inch Velma in floating blonde tresses and a mermaid suit made my jaw drop and my mind boggle. Full-size 3D Velma doing a weightless dance in a water tank was a whole other kettle of fish. Specifically, two enormous tits with a gold starfish on each nipple.

I'd thought I would switch off between watching her and filming her, but one look and I braced my back against the wall to hold my camera still.

She'd warned me you can't hold a conversation in a water tank. She would have to talk him through this before...

"Hey, babe!" Footsteps came down the stairs. Crossed the floor. Stopped. I heard a gasp. "Oh, fuck!"

Had he seen me?

"Holy fucking Jesus!"

No, he'd seen Velma.

"Where do I—? How do I—?"

His voice had dropped from tenor to baritone and thickened so he could hardly squeeze out words. Or maybe he'd quit trying. Loud splashes meant Velma was clinging to the rim of the tank.

"Nico! You came!"

"Any minute," he choked. "Let me touch you! Where can I—?"

"On the side. See the ladder? Climb on up."

"I don't—think I—"

"Sure you can." More splashing. "I can't come down in this tail. You gotta come up."

Clanging feet on metal rungs.

"No, stop! Take off your shoes. In fact, take off everything. No clothes in the tank. Easier if you strip down there."

"If I..?"

"Don't you want to swim naked with me? Stroke my fins? Curl your legs around my tail?"

Strangled noises mingled with the soft sharp sounds of his handmade Italian shoes and pret-a-porter jacket flying across the little room.

"Nibble my starfish? Come on, Nico. You ever fuck a mermaid?"

He was panting hard as a hound dog.

Swish-plop! "Hey! Careful!"

I hoped he'd missed the video cameras.

"Tha-a-t's it. Go-o-od boy. Ooh! What's that I see? Is that a worm?"

Muffled metallic ringing: he was climbing the ladder.

"Yum yum! Fishies like wormies! You know what I'm gonna do? Ooh! It's so big! I don't know if I can fit that big worm in my little mouth!"

A long shuddering groan from Nico. I sympathized. What's that old saying about the worm turns?

"Now, we're going in the water. You ready? Okay, listen. See this zipper? It goes both ways. Down to let me out, and up so I can pee. See, I'm zipping open the bottom. And when you and me are swimming, I'm gonna arch my tail, like this, and you're gonna wrap your legs around me and stick that nice big worm right, in, there."

He whimpered. Or maybe I did.

"Let's take off this starfish, so you can... Ooh, yeah!"

I focused every cell in my body on my camera. Hold the phone rock steady. Stand on that X exactly where my shot matches the mirrors. What mirrors? Don't ask. Don't make a sound. I am recording Nico Benedetto being unfaithful to his wife. Very, very, important. If I think about anything else, I could fuck this up, and Velma will never— Forget Velma. Think about Archer. My partner. Star of an upscale jazz combo who turned himself into a scruffy old street musician to save his band. To save his bass player, Joelle, the woman he loves. We're doing this to free Joelle from Nico, who doesn't love her because he'll never divorce her, but he might kill her, and if I think about mermaids or starfish, Joelle's murder will be my fault. Focus on the camera. Stand on the X. Total silence until the job's done. Not much longer. Half hour? Then I can face Archer again. Not Velma. I can never face Velma again. Forget Velma. Think about Archer. Focus on the camera.

I'd shut out the moaning and splashing sounds when they tumbled off the platform into the tank. Now I heard nothing. Just the soft burble of water.

I lowered my camera and peered through the hole in the folding screen.

For three seconds I saw a weird cameo of writhing arms and legs, a long green scaly tail, and a cloud of blonde hair. Drowning? No such luck. Velma's tail was arched, her plastic tresses hid Nico's face, and the only hand I could see was clasped tight over her left tit. His hips pumped as if he were trying to thrust, as she'd directed, but the water was slowing his momentum.

Red lights flashed on. What now, for fuck's sake? Fire? Not in a concrete bunker around a water tank. Why was the room blinking like a fire engine?

Nico jerked backward, sending out a burst of bubbles and raising his hair in black needles that stuck out like porcupine quills.

He surfaced, and his hair flattened, and I stepped off my X so he wouldn't see me.

A letterbox screen lit up beside the tank.

Velma's head popped up. "Hey! Nico! Why'd you stop?"

He looked around and hollered, "What the fuck is that?"

"Lights, what do you think? Are you okay? Your breathing tube—"

He slapped her hand away. Naked, splayed against the plexiglass with a massive hard-on, he looked like a fiddler crab.

"What the fuck is going on?"

"It's midnight, ding-dong! Last show! The lights mean we're coming through fine upstairs. If you look at the monitor—"

"Are you shitting me?"

"Actually, I was fucking you," she retorted. "But, you know, I can't do it by myself."

"Who are those people?" He jabbed his finger at the screen.

"Our audience. Damn good for a Thursday."

"Turn it off! Turn this all off!" He scrambled around the tank's rim, groping for the ladder.

I reached for my Beretta but reconsidered. There was no direction I could see this going that would make me shoot a naked man engaged in consensual underwater sex with a woman in a mermaid costume. Especially not if the woman was bait on a hook to catch the adulterer in flagrante.

Not with a Beretta, anyhow.

I stepped back onto the X and aimed my cell camera through the peephole again.

That's how I missed the crucial moment when Nico Benedetto was caught in flagrante by his own treacherous heart.

The resulting splash in the news media was too big to need repeating here. I'll only say that it was one of those rare times when the interests of all parties coincided. The backers of Nico's restaurant chain and the management of Bingo's Lounge issued a joint press release full of hoopla for them both (prize-winning tomato sauce, new gelateria, international tourist destination, legendary mermaid show) without any details that might embarrass the Benedetto family. Joelle traded an hour of X-rated video footage for her and Nico's house in North Beach, his vineyard in Sonoma, two cars, and full custody of the kids, who would grow up believing their dad died in their mom's arms on the dance floor. Archer said no to her offer of Nico's Porsche but yes to a year's contract for Thursday nights at Bingo's. The firm of Spade and Archer accepted a check that promised to keep Sarafina's in Chianti and Velma in health insurance for the next decade. Velma agreed not to pester us for new office furniture if we upgraded our computers and gave her a raise.

"Anything else?" I asked her, over coffee at Sarafina's two weeks later.

"Yeah." She licked her spoon. "Look at me."

I did a quick inspection, from her topiary haircut to her triple earrings to her baggy gray sweatshirt. "What?"

"My eyes."

"Have they changed?"

"No. You have. When I look at you, you always look away."

"Huh," I said.

"Like you're not curious anymore. You've seen it all. You think."

"I don't." Want to have this conversation.

"So, ask me a question."

"Like what?

"Aren't you scared you'll drown? How do you go to the bathroom? Have you ever had sex as a mermaid?"

"Velma..."

"Sometimes, I don't, and no. Never."

"I've never seen you scared of anything. I have seen you, as a mermaid, seduce a man. Two, if you count the one holding the camera."

"See, that's the thing. I was scared shitless when Nico's heart stopped. You helped me pull him out of there and do CPR. You held me until I stopped shaking. You could have fucked me coming and going, you know? And you didn't even look me in the eye."

"I didn't know..." How to touch a voluptuous naked woman with a fish's tail.

"Sex in the mermaid suit? You saw. It's practically impossible." She wrinkled her nose at her reflection in the spoon. "I took it on for you. This job. Spade and Archer. For Joelle, who I met at work and saw she was drowning. And Archer, who pulled her out."

"That's what we do," I said. "One way or another. Pull people out."

She lowered her spoon. "What about me? What about you?"

I looked at her fingers, her swimmer's arms, her pontoon tits floating like a life raft under her sweatshirt. I looked at her crimson lips. I looked into her eyes.

"What about Thursday night?" I said. "Think your mermaid suit'll be dry?"

She winked at me. "Bite my tail, Spade."

The Law of Stephanie
Albert Tucher

Diana glanced to her left. Tom Bradshaw was driving like a man running late for a job interview. Five miles faster, and she would have to give him a scolding. Clients often liked that anyway.

But her side-eye worked, and he eased off the gas.

"Women named Stephanie are always hot," he said. "Ever notice that?"

She thought about it, and damned if he didn't have a point. Some clients insisted on showing her pictures of their wives. She could recall three Stephanies who made her wonder why the men came to her.

Tom's mission tonight was to meet the ultimate Stephanie, and for that, he needed a wingman.

Woman, actually.

He turned left off the highway and ventured into the bedroom community of Lakeview. After ten years of seeing clients here, Diana still got lost among the McMansions that were pushing the last vestiges of the 1970s out of the far north of New Jersey. It was a relief to let someone else navigate.

Many of the new monstrosities hunkered on lots barely big enough to hold them. The house he selected had several acres of land and a long crescent driveway. A rent-a-cop waved Tom and his Lexus toward a parking spot between two upscale SUVs.

"Usual ground rules?" Diana asked.

He took the hint and pointed at the glove compartment. She removed an envelope and stowed it in her bag.

"You're my girlfriend, if anyone asks. You go your way, I go mine.

At some point, you have to give it up to at least a couple of the guys. Or the gals, as you prefer."

"You know I don't do women."

"Up to you. Just be nice about saying no. Then we go back to my place and finish up."

"I've done swinger parties before."

"I know. I just hope I can get next to Stephanie. She's going to be popular."

He grinned.

"First, she's going to provide entertainment. Did I mention that women cellists are also hot? Put a Stephanie and a cello together, things go nuclear."

"Call it the Law of Stephanie."

Other guests were getting out of their vehicles and approaching the house. Everyone looked dressed to undress. Diana wore a shirt-dress over nothing.

A blonde woman in her forties, naked except for stiletto heels, stood just inside the front door.

"Tom, good to see you."

"Thanks for having us, Rebecca. This is Diana."

"And this is my husband Leclair."

Diana put it together. This husband must be a recent acquisition. With his receding gray hair and abundant waistline, he wasn't bringing sex appeal to the partnership.

The house was a broad hint his contribution was money.

"We're getting undressed right away," said Rebecca. "Use the sun room through there, and we'll start in fifteen minutes."

Diana made her living getting naked with strangers, but usually one at a time. She would never admit it, but swinger parties didn't come up often enough to get her accustomed to this much skin. Some of the naked bodies were pleasant to behold, but many weren't, which perversely reminded her of clients and helped settle her down.

The huge living room cut through the second floor and went all the way up to the roof. The room held more sofas and love seats than a furniture store. The hosts had supplemented the permanent items with several dozen folding chairs, set up to face one more chair at the far end of the room.

"Let's sit close," said Diana on impulse.

Whatever was about to happen, she wanted a good view.

Tom agreed. They took two chairs, which fortunately had padding and skin-friendly fabric instead of bare wood or metal.

Guests began to fill the other seats. Rebecca walked up and stopped by the lone chair.

"I've been wondering what to say, but I realized you all know what to expect. Introductions are unnecessary, so please welcome Stephanie."

Naked people all joining in a round of applause looked a little weird. Maybe there was a point to clothes.

A woman emerged from a doorway behind Rebecca. Tom was right. This woman had to be a Stephanie, and she carried a large stringed instrument and a bow.

And, of course, she was naked.

Stephanie's dark and dramatic coloring made Diana think she might as well pull on jeans and a sweatshirt.

The cellist took her seat in the folding chair and rested the instrument beside her on the little spike. She parted her thighs in a cellist's usual posture, but cellists don't usually play naked. Diana decided she might as well take a professional look at the area Stephanie seemed determined to display.

Trimmed but not shaved. Check. Something they had in common.

Distinctly aroused. There Stephanie had gotten ahead of her.

Stephanie met Diana's eyes for a challenging moment. She lifted her instrument with one hand. When she maneuvered the cello between her knees, the negligent strength of the gesture gave Diana a tingle down below.

She leaned close to Tom.

"You're welcome."

He grinned.

"Good idea, getting close."

Stephanie tested her tuning with a couple of brief strokes, paused, and began to play.

Authority. That was the word.

Diana knew authority when she heard it, whether it came from a talking head on television, or a cop who commanded obedience because he admitted no alternative.

When a performer, naked or not, seemed to take dictation straight from a heavenly library of music, authority was the word.

The low notes sawed at Diana's core. The high notes told any violinists on the premises they weren't needed. The fleet passages made her wriggle with delight, while the sustained sections stung her eyes with tears.

The naked people who rose to applaud no longer looked strange.

"Paganini," said Tom into her ear. "Rebecca told me. Originally for violin. On the cello, it's even more of a feat."

"There must be a story about her," said Diana.

Tom started to answer, but Stephanie held up her hand for silence. The audience settled in their seats. Stephanie laid her instrument on its side on the carpet and crossed her legs. Diana would have thought it was a little late for a demure act, but Stephanie made the gesture work. She looked around the audience, and her eyes settled on Diana.

"Tonight you're mine," she said.

A thousand dollars, Diana thought.

That was the amount in Tom's envelope. She was earning it all in this moment. It was nowhere near enough for what she had to do, and she would find out what kind of man he was the next time they discussed money.

"Thanks," she said. "But my boyfriend would never forgive me."

She laid her hand on Tom's shoulder.

"He's yours for as long as you want him."

Stephanie maintained her smile, but Diana had closed off that opportunity forever. Stephanie stood and held her hand out to Tom. The other party-goers applauded as they had for the music, as the couple made for the stairs.

Rebecca reappeared.

"Now it's time for us. Let's play."

For Diana, play was work. She walked and watched and tried to look fascinated, as amateurs did for fun what she did on the clock.

Three middle-aged women tried things they should have done twenty years earlier when they had the flexibility to make them go. One of the women caught sight of Diana and started to invite her into the tangle of limbs. Diana smiled and turned to make a graceful escape, but an arm snaked around her waist. She stifled her urge to shake off the arm. Leclair smiled down at her.

"Shall we go upstairs?"

"Isn't privacy against the rules?"

"I make the rules."

"You don't want Stephanie?"

"I'll see her later. One of the perks."

"Okay."

Tom would be impressed she had earned her payday with the host himself. Leclair led her up a curved staircase. Diana looked around and caught his wife watching. The woman smiled and nodded, but Diana's instincts wouldn't let her accept anything like that at face value.

She also didn't care for it when he pulled her into the master bedroom. He read her expression.

"My wife likes the used sheets."

"If you say so."

She gave the layout a quick professional inspection. The room was built on the same scale as the rest of the house. That was good. If he had a weapon in a drawer or the bathroom, getting to it would cost him crucial seconds.

A smart hooker considered the hazards and mapped out an escape route.

"I wanted you the moment you came in," he said. "Almost-beautiful women like you are the most beautiful in the long run."

Other men had made the same point, but seldom with such elegance.

"Not that you're going to turn Stephanie down," she said.

He smiled.

"Of course not. I'm not going to spill your secret, either."

"My secret?"

"Tom brought you because we don't admit solo men to our parties. Paid companions are against the rules."

"How did you know?"

She saw no point in denying it.

"I saw you at the Savoy."

What he had been doing at the premiere hot-pillow motel in the far north of New Jersey wasn't her business.

"But it's okay. I would never have guessed otherwise. Stephanie definitely didn't. I saw your little interaction."

Someone had already turned the bedclothes down. Diana imagined a domestic helper performing the chore and sneering inwardly at the reasons. She lay back on the luxuriant sheets and felt inspired to perform a Stephanie spread.

Maybe she would call it that from now on.

Leclair climbed on and began thrusting into her, but as his climax approached, he slowed and pulled out.

"That's one thing I can't get used to about these parties," she said as his breathing returned to normal. "Most guys come to me to get off."

"What's the line from that movie?

"Emanuelle," said Diana.

He wasn't the first man to bring it up.

"'The definition of true love is the erection, not the orgasm.' I've come to agree."

"I'm not sure it makes much sense."

"It doesn't have to," he said. "It's French."

He rolled onto his back. His erection pointed toward the ceiling, impressive for a man of his age and physical condition. She reached over and stroked him in his condom, but she was thinking about another movie from years ago. It was something French, but she couldn't quite come up with it. Why did it seem important?

"As a practical matter, most men my age are one and done," he added. "Kinda poops the party."

"So we have some time," said Diana. "Tell me about Stephanie."

"The most famous cellist you've never heard of."

"Not that I've heard of many. Yo Yo Ma."

"She could be bigger than Yo Yo Ma. She has the chops, and just look at her. That's the definition of cross-over appeal. She could even spin this swinger hobby of hers into something fascinating."

"But?"

"She came out of Juilliard a few years ago. Conductors and agents were all lined up, ready to duel to the death over her. She played a concert in London and one in Tokyo, and then she quit. Said she lived for the music, but the business would kill her in a year."

"So instead she does fuck parties?"

"She doesn't have to make sense either. Not looking like that."

"She has to pay the bills. Does she sell records?"

"She doesn't believe in recording."

He hesitated for a second.

"She comes from money. She doesn't even have to get out of bed."

"You know a lot about her."

"It's frustrating. Concerts are my business."

He sat up with some effort, and she took her hand away.

"I should get back to my host gig," he said.

She followed and stopped beside him at the top of the stairs. She pointed up at the ceiling.

"Pretty state-of-the-art. I assume they're turned off for this occasion?"

"Sharp eye."

"Occupational hazard. I always check for cameras."

"They're off. I promise."

They leaned on the banister and watched the scene below them. The party sprawled across the enormous living room. One man had lined three women up on a sofa with their legs in the air, as he went up and down the row, penetrating each woman for a dozen strokes before going on to the next.

And back again.

"Lucky Lucy in the middle there," said Diana. "That guy must really have his line working to get three of them."

There were never enough women to go around at these parties, even with the rule against single men, because many of the women came for women.

Diana descended the stairs and wandered into the scrum, and soon she was on her back on the new carpet, looking up at a man she knew even less about than the average client. For a few minutes she tried to guess his life story, but the topic didn't hold her interest.

The man rolled off her, and a wiry, balding man took his place without consulting her. She decided not to make an issue. He was number three for the evening, one more than her deal with Tom required. When this man was done with her, she could find someplace to hide with a clear conscience.

Fifteen minutes later she found her way to the restaurant-grade kitchen. A woman old enough to be Diana's mother sat naked at the breakfast bar with a cup of coffee in front of her.

"Better than sex," said Diana

The woman opened her mouth to argue or agree when the scream came.

"What's that?" The older woman demanded.

Diana was already on the move. Her destination was the sunroom and her shirtdress. She needed to get dressed because she knew what police business sounded like.

Then she went back to the kitchen for the heavenly coffee. Even if she could round Tom up with the car keys, fleeing the house was not an option. She knew who would come, and if he had to track her down, he would make her pay.

"Someday I'm gonna let a bad guy get away with it," said Breitwieser. "Just to put the cuffs on you."

Diana sat on one of the folding chairs in the living room. The detective stood over her and gave her his cop glare. He had a pretty good one, but he should have learned by now it didn't work on her.

"I'm still your favorite hooker, though."

She also wouldn't mind if he surprised her by losing some weight or his comb over, or improving on his polyester suits. She drained her coffee and thought about going for more, but that would provoke him a bit too much. He might cuff her just for fun.

"I'm surprised you stuck around," he said.

"Can't we skip the preliminaries? You're not surprised I stuck around, because we've done this dance before."

As she trash-talked him, she watched his investigative machine in action. Some of the partygoers seemed to have escaped the premises, knocking chairs over as they ran, but the cops still had quite a few guests to question. Breitwieser had several uniformed officers inspect naked people for blood or wounds and then escort them two at a time to the sunroom, where they could dress for their role as witnesses.

"So this is one of those sex parties," said Breitwieser.

"You must be a detective."

"Not your scene, I wouldn't think. Sex for fun, I mean."

"This is business."

She explained the couples rule.

"A lot of guys don't have a woman they can talk into doing this."

"And you were working for this Tom Bradshaw tonight."

She hesitated.

"Relax. I don't care about that right now."

"Okay, it was Tom."

He paused, and she looked around. Rebecca had pulled a robe on, and she sat on the same sofa where the lone man had serviced the three women. She looked stunned and haggard, but finding her husband butchered in their bedroom accounted for that. A uniformed officer watched her.

Stephanie occupied the other end of the same sofa. She wore sweats and a bored expression. Somehow she still looked glamorous.

"She look like a killer to you?" Breitwieser asked.

"Which?"

It didn't surprise Diana he fell right into bouncing ideas off her. Their shared history included a fair amount of informal collaboration.

He would deny it, of course.

"The wife," he said.

"With all these people around?"

"Makes for a lot of alternate suspects."

"Blood on her?"

"The killer showered off in the master bathroom. Convenient everybody was already naked."

"What was the weapon?"

"Barber's professional scissors from the bathroom."

Diana hadn't seen the blood or the body, but that detail made Leclair's murder real. She had just been thinking about potential weapons in that bathroom.

"What's the motive?" she asked.

"Jealousy."

"They're swingers."

"Maybe they found out they couldn't handle it."

"Their marriage is pretty new," said Diana, "but I got the impression they've done this before."

"There's always the money motive. Place like this, I'll bet they're underwater. I see it all the time."

"So, life insurance?"

"I'll definitely check."

"I'm with you on the money motive. It doesn't have to be life insurance, though."

"Then what?"

"I've been trying to remember something all night. It just came to me."

She explained.

"Let's find out," he said.

He called a uniformed officer over and conferred. The young man nodded and departed. Diana watched him climb the stairs and disappear.

"He's our techie," said Breitwieser to Diana.

They waited for twenty minutes, neither feeling a need to converse. The officer reappeared at the top of the stairs and called, "I found it. Like you said."

Diana decided not to claim credit.

"I can get her to talk," she said instead.

Breitwieser made up his mind in seconds, proving once again the dull, plodding cop routine was an act.

"It won't work if we do it here," he said.

"I think you're right."

"We'll have to take the other one in for questioning. At least make it look like we're arresting her."

"You'll need to tell me the details from the crime scene. So I get it right when I talk to her."

"I'll fill you in."

"You're going to owe me," she said.

"Forget it."

"I'm serious. If I get enough for an arrest, I don't want any cop hassles in your territory."

Breitwieser's body language said they had a deal. He would deny its existence, but he would keep it, at least for a while. Then they would start over, again and again, until the day one of them retired.

* * *

"I'm breaking my own rule," said Stephanie.

"Wearing clothes?" said Diana.

They had consulted their closets and both came out with business casual black pants and conservative tops in shades of blue. Stephanie ignored the lame joke.

"No, agreeing to meet you. Somebody turns me down, they don't usually get another chance. You're different."

Stephanie studied her openly.

"You're almost beautiful in a way that's very beautiful. I'm sure you've heard that before."

"More or less. Tell me why you live up here in the boonies."

"I don't like New York any more than I like the concert scene."

"But you have no connections here, do you?"

"That's exactly why I chose it."

Stephanie looked around Rosen's restaurant.

"I've passed this place, but I've never been inside. It has a certain raffish charm."

Her condescension made Diana want to defend her favorite hangout.

The waitress delivered her hamburger deluxe, but Diana let it sit. Her appetite had fled. This meeting had several possible outcomes, none of them good.

Stephanie hadn't even ordered food.

"So, what are we talking about?" she asked.

"Strategy," said Diana. "Rebecca didn't kill him. The cops will figure that out, and then we're both in for it. Because we were in that bedroom."

"How do you know I was there?"

"Leclair told me you were next on his to-do list. He pulled out of me to save his pop shot for you."

Diana pictured him blissed out on the bed, while Stephanie went to the bathroom to find the scissors.

"You have a certain bluntness about bodily functions that I would call professional," said Stephanie.

"Good catch."

"Tom is not your boyfriend."

"Hardly."

"So you didn't mind when I sent him home spent."

"I got paid."

"He performed three times, which for his age is impressive."

"I'm sure you know you can inspire greatness." Diana stopped herself from making a face. It was an occupational hazard to take verbal cues from the men who paid her, but Stephanie wasn't a client. Diana didn't need to sound like her.

On the other hand, it might help her get what she needed.

"Tom told me," she said. "He was very proud of himself."

She took a breath.

"And that's not all he told me."

"Really."

Stephanie's face became a mask.

"He said he mentioned Leclair's sound system to you. Rebecca told him about it. State of the art, like the video."

"I suppose it stands to reason, but it never occurred to me."

"But you knew about it when you went to see him in the master bedroom."

"And what difference does that make?"

"Diva."

Stephanie blinked.

"It's a French movie," said Diana. "Leclair was into French films. In my line of work, I have to pick up fast on what a man is into. Then I'm into it too, for an hour at a time. Anyway, Leclair liked French movies. I haven't seen many, but I have seen Diva."

Now was the time to bore in.

"Do you know it? It's about a singer who refuses to record. Like you."

Stephanie gave her nothing.

"What's your issue with recording?"

"It's part of the music business. I don't want any of it."

"Leclair was part of it too. He had a state-of-the-art security system. That means cameras and sound. You went into that bedroom knowing the cameras were off, but the sound was on. You knew he recorded you like the young guy in the movie. How did Leclair spin it? I figure he would play the recording for you and try to persuade you to let him sell it. Did you try just telling him no before you stabbed him?"

"No."

"No, what? You didn't tell him no, or you didn't stab him?"

"It never occurred to me for a second he would listen to me. One thing I've learned. Men don't take no."

"The law of Stephanie," said Diana.

"It should be your law too."

That one hit hard. Diana wanted to take it all back and tell Breitwieser the deal was off. She opened her mouth to speak into the microphone between her breasts.

She was too late. Over Stephanie's shoulder Diana saw Breitwieser and two uniformed officers come out of the kitchen. Diana had only a moment to ask one last thing.

"How was killing him supposed to help? The recording still exists."

"How the hell should I know? I just make the music. Is that detective coming?"

"Yes."

"Before he gets here, did they find the condom? Did I leave prints anywhere?"

"No."

"So they'd have had nothing without this. Figures. What do you get out of it?"

And Diana, who never wilted under a cop's glare or any man's, found she couldn't meet Stephanie's eyes.

"I'm asking myself the same thing."

Concerto for Harp and Homicide
Shari Held

"There's no religion but sex and music."

- Sting

"I can't believe we have to lug Hannigan's harp all the way up to the seventh floor," Billy Martin said as he helped heft the harp onto the trolley.

"I can't believe Conductor Marx lets that womanizing little prick get away with all his prima donna demands," his coworker said. "Hannigan must have something on him. He plays the harp like an angel, but he's got more in common with the devil."

The symphony had begun its annual outreach tour of free concerts in small towns whose residents wouldn't otherwise be able to attend a professional performance. It was Billy's job to ensure all the equipment was accounted for and set up the facility to meet the symphony's needs.

Billy nodded. "Yeah. You can't imagine how tempted I am to drop his precious harp. Terpsichore, he calls it. His muse." He snickered. "I'd like to break its strings. Smash it up good. Oopsie!" He shook his head. "After all the grief Hannigan's given me for being gay, the bastard deserves it."

"Speak of the devil."

Harry Hannigan rushed toward them. "Easy, now," the harp virtuoso shouted. "Be careful. She's delicate." He winced when Billy "accidentally" plucked Terpsichore's strings as they entered the service elevator. "For god's sake, touch the strings again and you'll be one dead queer."

* * *

Once the harp was safely ensconced in his hotel room, Harry dressed for dinner. At ten, one of his groupies–"Missy," "Millie," some M-word–would join him in his room. He hadn't hooked up with her before, at least not that he remembered. She wasn't exactly in the same class as J-Lo, but she'd do for a couple nights of fun until they got back to civilization. Who knows? Maybe she'd be the one who could replace Terpsichore as his muse.

* * *

Millie Mason couldn't believe her luck. She was spending the night with her idol, Harry Hannigan of the thick black hair, sparkling blue eyes, and rakish grin. She would savor every kiss. Every caress. Every spine-tingling erotic moment.

With Harry's usual adoring gaggle of groupies back in the city, Millie had hit the jackpot. The thought of Harry's hands playing her body like they played his harp, sent waves of warmth washing over her. If merely thinking about it produced this sensation, what would the real thing be like?

Millie trembled. One night with her and Harry would realize they belonged together. He'd stop his philandering ways and settle down with her. She was sure of it. She fastened the thin gold chain with the harp charm around her neck. Her good luck charm. She'd worn it the first time she'd seen Harry in concert and every day since. The harp was the symbol of Saint Cecilia, patron saint of musicians. When worn as jewelry, it symbolized hope. Millie really got into symbolism. She was big on hope, too.

She checked herself in the mirror. Not bad. Her cornflower dress made her brown eyes dance and her stilettos did fantastic things for her legs. She applied Strawberry Shimmer gloss on her lips and headed for Harry's room.

He answered at the second knock. "Whoa, look at you," he said.

Millie blushed and became tongue-tied. That didn't matter. Harry covered her hand with his, led her to the loveseat in the room's sitting area, and poured them each a glass of wine. He stared into her eyes as they toasted. "To a beautiful woman and a beautiful evening," he said and leaned toward her.

A subtle mix of sandalwood, musk, and man emanated from Harry's skin. Millie didn't object when he unzipped her dress, pulled it down, and unfastened her bra so he could fondle her breasts. Her nipples became hard and erect as he applied more pressure and began to tease them with his tongue. Millie closed her eyes and enjoyed the sensations that coursed through her body.

"Let's take it nice and slow, enjoy the anticipation," Harry whispered as he released her, poured the remainder of the wine, and called room service for another bottle.

Millie stood and slipped out of her dress and bra. She sat on Harry's lap and ran her fingers through his hair while he moistened one finger with wine and ran it ever so slowly over her areolas. She moaned, oblivious to anything but the intensity of her feelings.

She drained her glass of wine. "I think you're simply wonderful," she said in a breathy wisp of a voice she didn't recognize as her own. "I've wanted this for so long."

Harry put his arms around Millie, pulled her tight against his body, then pressed his mouth against hers with an urgency she reciprocated. His tongue pushed past her lips and slid into her mouth.

"Let's move into the other room," he said when they pulled apart, his voice husky. He kissed her again and gently squeezed her ass. She quivered and leaned against him for support as they arose and moved as one into the bedroom.

Millie was surprised to see his harp set up in one corner. She reached her hand toward it but he rushed in front of her and grabbed it. "Please, don't touch the harp," he said.

A sharp rap on the door signaled room service. "Excuse me. I'll be right back."

Millie couldn't resist running her fingers over the harp. To her horror, a string broke with a loud pop. "Oh," she gasped, jumping back. Fortunately, the break coincided with the uncorking of the wine. She didn't want anything to spoil the moment, so when Harry returned, she didn't mention it.

"Now, where were we?" Harry asked after he poured the wine. "Ah, just about here." He moved her hand to his groin. "I want to feel you caress me. Make love to my cock. But first..." He undressed in thirty-seconds-flat.

With a wantonness she hadn't known she possessed, Millie knelt and took his throbbing cock in her mouth, teased it with her tongue, and slid the shaft in and out of her moist, soft mouth. Harry placed his hands on her shoulders, pulled her close to match her rhythm, to drive his cock deeper into her mouth. Millie sensed he was near release, so she pulled back and stood to explore the texture of the skin on his torso. First with her fingertips. Then with her tongue. Harry shivered.

He pulled down her lace panties and she stepped out of them. Their naked bodies ground together like they merged into one. A warm sensation traveled down Millie's body and culminated in the area between her legs. She could feel it grow moist in anticipation.

Harry pushed Millie on the bed, then got on his knees and began to stimulate her with his tongue. She moaned and squirmed in ecstasy. When his tongue lightly brushed across her vagina, she was caught in a whirlwind of emotion so strong she thought she would die. She shuddered and convulsed with pleasure.

Harry straddled her, leaned over her, thrust his cock in her mouth. It grew and stiffened as she sucked it. Tasting him. Feeling its smoothness and wondering what it would feel like inside her.

They were on the same wavelength. Harry pulled out, placed his arms beneath her hips, and plunged his cock into her sweet wetness. He thrust harder and harder. Without mercy. Millie didn't want mercy. She wanted Harry. All of him. "Oh, god, Harry," she moaned. "I love you."

"I love you, too, sweetheart," he panted. Their lovemaking rose to a crescendo that climaxed in an explosive release.

* * *

Eight o'clock in the morning. Harry awoke and looked at Millie. It was tempting to lie here and play with her all day. Instead, he sent her off to her room with a promise to take her to lunch later.

At breakfast, Harry bumped into Sean and Fiona Ryan. He wasn't sure if he should classify them as friend or foe since their last meeting hadn't ended on a high note. Harry had beat out Sean for the symphony position. Sean was good—better than Harry actually, but Harry caught Conductor Marx "making music" with the first violinist and used the info to his advantage. Now, Sean taught music to high school students in some Podunk town. That was a friendship killer.

However, Harry still had fond memories of the beautiful Fiona, his old flame. When she approached his table, he turned on the charm. "Please, sit," Harry said. "Long time, no see. What have you two been up to? Any kiddos?"

Fiona blushed. "No kids. Sean's still teaching." She looked at Sean who sat beside her. He grunted and looked down at his shoes.

Harry couldn't resist needling him. "Still haven't gotten over the fact I beat you out for the symphony position, eh, Sean?"

Sean jerked up from his chair, almost colliding with their waitress. "You mean the position you stole from me?"

"Admit it. You're jealous I'm getting standing ovations, while you're stuck in some god-forsaken town teaching snot-nosed little kids. But, hey, you won Fiona. I'd say we're even."

Everyone in the dining room strained to get an earful without appearing to eavesdrop. The room was so quiet, Harry's words reached them all.

"You know, I'd be nice to me if I were you," Harry said. "I hear about numerous jobs. I could get you gigs to help get you back in circulation."

"Wouldn't that be wonderful, honey?" Fiona grabbed Sean's hand. When she received no response, she turned toward Harry. "Well, thank you for thinking of us."

The waitress dropped the bill on the table and scurried away. Harry charged it to his room and made sure everyone noticed he left a big tip.

"Come on, Fiona." Sean grabbed her arm and propelled her toward the elevator.

Harry headed to the elevator too. He ignored the waves of malice Sean emitted and took Fiona's hand in his on the pretext of admiring her bracelet. "Very pretty, but not as pretty as you." There, that ought to piss off Sean big time.

They piled into the elevator and both men punched the button for the seventh floor. It was a long, slow, silent ride.

Harry walked to his door and noticed Sean and Fiona stopped two doors down.

Once inside his room, Harry laughed. He'd never understand how he ended up with Fiona. Sean never did have a sense of humor.

Harry flexed his long, slim fingers. Keeping them limber was essential to his performance. He sat by his harp and ran his fingers over the strings. What? A broken string? Terpsichore was in perfect shape last night at rehearsal. Sometime between then and now, someone violated her. He could replace the string, but she wouldn't play up to his exacting standards in time for the performance. Someone tried to sabotage his performance! He'd bet it was that good-for-nothing Sean.

Harry flung his door wide open, stormed to Sean and Fiona's room, and pounded on their door. He didn't pay attention to the couple waiting for the elevator or the maid at the end of the hall. He beat on the door until Fiona opened it.

"Harry. What's wrong?" Fiona asked.

Harry brushed her aside and strode toward Sean, grabbed him by the shoulder, and shoved him. "What the hell have you done to my harp?"

"What the hell are you talking about?" Sean asked and pushed back.

"Stop it." Fiona tried to get between them. "Harry, mind your hands."

"His hands?" Sean said. "What about my hands?"

Fiona ignored Sean. "Harry, whatever you think Sean did, I can assure you, he didn't. He's been with me since we arrived last night. Now, what's got you so riled up?"

Harry backed off. "My string. Someone broke one of my strings.

Terpsichore won't play the same in time for the concert."

"Good!" Sean said. "Whoever did it, more power to them."

Fiona put her arm around Harry and led him toward the door. "Sean didn't mean that," she whispered. "It's just, well, he's under a lot of pressure right now."

Harry glanced back at Sean, who appeared to be engrossed in a TV show. "You want to come back to my room?" Harry asked Fiona. "You can tell me all about it then."

Fiona nodded and grabbed her beach bag. "Sean, I'm going for a swim." She slipped out the door behind Harry and they entered his room.

"I'd offer you a stiff one, but it's still rather early—even for me," Harry said.

"It's never too early for a stiff one," Fiona purred. "Isn't that what you told me back in the day when we were an item?" She placed a hand on his crotch. "I've missed you, Harry."

Harry's cock sprung to life. "Evidently, I've missed you, too." He wrapped his arms around her and kissed her, then led her to the bed. "Are you sure about this?"

"More than anything," Fiona shed her clothes and threw herself on the bed. "I've always loved you, Harry. It should have been you. Not Sean. I know that now. Make love to me like you used to."

Harry didn't need to be told twice. Their passion was fast and furious. Afterward, they lay there, two old lovers. He caressed her bare skin. He briefly wondered if she was that passionate with Sean. He dismissed the thought. Of course, she wasn't.

"I love you, Harry," she said.

"I love you, too," he said, still in the afterglow of sex. Fiona stroked his cock, willing it back to action with all the magic she had in her fingertips until Harry laid his hands on hers to stop her.

"I think I'm going to leave Sean. I thought maybe you and I could… reconnect. What do you think?"

Harry noticed lines around her eyes that hadn't been there before.

That her skin wasn't as taut. Her eyes not as bright and carefree. He released her hands and stood to deliver his rejection.

"We're really good together, aren't we," Harry?" Fiona asked, a hint of desperation in her voice.

"We were. A long time ago. But you made your choice. Now we're just... old lovers. Nothing more. You'd better get back to Sean."

"You said you loved me," Fiona said.

"I do. I love every woman I've ever been with romantically. At the time, anyway. Once, I did think about settling down with you. It wouldn't have worked out. Believe me."

Fiona pleaded with him and cursed him in turn. He'd forgotten what a shrew she could be. He needed a drink.

He picked up the phone and ordered two mimosas from room service, then he noticed the time. Whoops! He'd have to get their drinks, make a toast, and hustle Fiona out of the room before Millie showed up for lunch.

"My dear, I'd love you to stay here with me, but I have things I need to attend to." He slapped her bottom. He hoped she'd take the hint and get a move on.

* * *

Right about then, Millie, one of the things Harry had to attend to, was poised to knock on Harry's door when Sean marched up to her.

"This is Harry Hannigan's room, right?" he asked Millie.

"Yes," Millie said. "Who are you?"

"An old, um, friend, here to see his concert," Sean said.

"Really? That's nice. I'm sure he'll want to see you." Millie knocked on the door.

Harry, who expected room service, answered wearing nothing but a towel. Sean burst through the door, shoved Millie aside and pushed Harry into the room.

"Where is she?" Sean said. "Where's my wife?" He strode across the room and opened the bedroom door.

Fiona had scrambled for her clothes when she heard Sean. She wasn't fast enough. "It's not what it looks like," she said.

Sean yanked her into the sitting room with Harry and Millie.

"Well, it sure as hell doesn't look like you were swimming. The only thing swimming is Harry's sperm. In your vagina. I bet you knew he'd be here when you signed us up for this weekend getaway. This was all a ruse to see your former lover. "

In the hallway, all eyes, including Billy's, were on the drama unfurling between Fiona and Sean. Harry managed to get into his pants and shout a derogatory comment to Billy.

"What are you looking at, you nosy little homo?"

Millie stayed rooted to the spot, not knowing what to do. She tried to rationalize the scene before her eyes, but no matter how creative she was, she couldn't spin it any other way. She'd been used. She'd been apart from Harry for less than six hours and he'd betrayed her. With an older, married woman. The vows of love he'd made to her meant nothing. No way she was going to warm his bed tonight. First thing tomorrow, she was out of here. Head down, she ran past a group of people who were getting a kick out of other people's misery.

* * *

The next morning found Marx fuming. Neither Harry's harp nor the harp virtuoso himself had shown up for rehearsal. He sent the second chair viola to Harry's room to check on him. No response. Marx was tired to death of Harry's shenanigans. After rehearsal, he finagled someone at the hotel desk to go with him to Harry's suite.

They knocked, then went inside. The sitting room was empty. "Harry, damnit, what's wrong with you?" Marx called out. "Why'd you miss rehearsal?" When he received no response, he stepped into the bedroom. Harry sprawled on the floor, Terpsichore on top of him. His face covered in blood.

"My god!" Marx turned to the desk clerk. "We have to contact the police. Or the sheriff. Whatever you have in this town."

The desk clerk looked like his breakfast was going to decorate the carpet. He locked the door behind them and they returned to the front desk.

A meeting of the local Rotary Club was just breaking up. The desk clerk pulled Deputy Hay aside. The three of them dashed to Harry's room.

"Looks like a homicide, all right," Deputy Hay said after he ascertained Harry was no longer among the living. "Did you two touch anything when you were in here?"

Both shook their heads.

"No selfies with the dead body or anything like that?"

They just stared at him.

"I have to ask. There's a lot of sickos out there who get off on stuff like that." He looked at the body again, then back to Marx. "Anybody in your orchestra have a beef with the deceased?"

Marx tried to muffle his laugh, which came out as a snort. "Harry wasn't exactly Mr. Popularity, but we're used to divas. I don't think anyone in the symphony would murder him." He shrugged his shoulders.

"Well, put the word out to all your folks, no one leaves this hotel until we've talked to them and they've been cleared." Deputy Hay turned toward the desk clerk. "That goes for anyone booked into the hotel. While the sheriff's out of town, I'll head the investigation. I'll secure the scene and notify my crew and the coroner. We'll start talking to people pretty darn soon."

* * *

By late afternoon, Deputy Hay had learned several facts. Eighty pounds of harp had slammed into Hannigan's left temple and killed him. From what he'd learned about Hannigan, it seemed like poetic justice.

No one had anything nice to say about the guy, other than he financially supported numerous charities and was active in fundraisers. Most never saw him except at rehearsals. All had opportunity, means, and perhaps motive, as well. Four people had closely interacted with Hannigan at the hotel.

He'd called Billy Martin politically incorrect names based on

Martin's sexual preference, ridiculed him in front of the entire symphony and others. No love lost there. Could Hannigan have maligned Billy one time too many?

Hannigan had two-timed Millie Mason, the young woman he'd been with Wednesday night. She appeared to alternate between grief from losing him and anger he'd been such a prick.

The Ryans had a history with Hannigan. In the space of one day, Sean Ryan had three altercations with Hannigan. Multiple people, with no relationship with either man, had witnessed each exchange.

As for Fiona Ryan, had her one-off fling with Hannigan ended on a good note or a sour one? Hannigan's beating out her husband for the symphony position seemed to bother her as much as it bothered her husband. Lost dreams, no matter if they were for a career or a lifestyle, were always a strong motive for murder.

He'd dig deeper before he'd accuse anyone. Let them sweat a bit. Delay was good for clearing the conscience.

* * *

That evening during cocktail hour, an unlikely group gathered around a table: Billy Martin, Millie Mason, and Sean and Fiona Ryan. Sean and Fiona didn't sit next to one another.

"I friggin' know that deputy thinks I did it because Hannigan called me a queer and hassled me," Billy said. "I usually keep how I feel about him inside. Tell myself he's not worth getting all riled up about. That nobody thinks that way but him. Yesterday, of all days, I chose to shoot my mouth off. Called him a bastard. Threatened to damage his harp. The guy helping me got an earful. I'm sure he spilled his guts to Deputy Hay."

"Do you have an alibi?" Fiona asked.

"Who knows?" Billy said. "They didn't tell me time of death. Did they say anything about it?"

Everyone shook their heads.

"I futzed around in the music hall that afternoon," Billy said. "Then, I walked around the town a bit. Ate here. Ended up going out for a beer or two at a pub. How about you, guys?"

Fiona piped up next. "Well, Sean and I had a big fight that afternoon, which I'm sure comes as no surprise to anyone here." She looked at Billy specifically.

"Um, right." Billy turned a shade of red that clashed with his peach Izod polo. "Word gets around, you know."

"After we fought, I went swimming, then booked a session at what the hotel refers to as its spa—manicure, pedicure, massage. That evening, I..." She looked at Sean. "I went to the movies and sat through a double feature before I went back to our room. I'm covered for the afternoon, but if he was killed later than that, not so much." She looked down at her shoes. "The movie was kind of a spur-of-the-moment thing. I didn't have cash or a card with me, so I sneaked in without buying a ticket. I'm screwed if he was murdered last night."

"You seem to get screwed a lot," Millie said, not quite under her breath.

"Now, wait a minute," Sean said.

Millie ignored him. "Why would the deputy suspect you?" Millie asked Fiona. "You seemed to be on very good terms with Harry."

All eyes turned to Fiona. She ran her tongue over her lips and addressed Sean rather than Millie. "Harry rejected me," Fiona spat out. "I had this illusion of the two of us getting together after all these years, but it's not what he wanted." She turned to Millie. "Harry enjoyed women but his harp was the only thing he truly loved. He'd never have given you another thought after he got back to the city." Fiona paused, a puzzled look on her face. "Speaking of harps, what happened to the antique harp charm you were wearing on that chain yesterday?"

Millie's hand went to her gold chain. "I took it off in tribute to Harry after he died. It was too painful to wear it." Her eyes filled with tears.

"Right," Fiona said. "I'm not buying it. You've got to be mad as hell that Harry screwed me, as you so bluntly put it, soon after you left his bed."

Millie's white-knuckled fingers clutched the table like she tried to restrain herself from directing a nasty retort to Fiona.

"Fiona, that's enough," Sean said.

"So, what's your alibi for yesterday?" Billy asked Millie.

"I was upset after the, um, incident," she said as she glanced at Fiona. "I went back to my room and pretty much indulged my misery for hours. Later that evening, I ordered a bottle of wine and some fries from room service. That's about it." Her face appeared to crumble.

Sean leaned back in his chair. "Well, I wouldn't worry. None of you have the honor of practically coming to blows with Hannigan—three times in one day, no less." The expression on his face didn't match the joking way he said it. "I was alone in the hotel room most of the day. Then, I visited a pub or two that night. Too bad we weren't at the same one, Billy. We could alibi each other."

Fiona shivered. "Isn't it weird to think the killer might be right here?"

They all jumped when Deputy Hay came from the next room and stood in front of their table. "So, you guys solved the case, already?"

His question provoked nervous laughter.

Sean was the first to leave. "I've got to talk to Marx about a gig filling in for Harry."

"I have to go to the front desk to see about getting a separate room," Fiona said.

The other two said nothing, got up, and went their separate ways.

* * *

Millie paced the floor in her hotel room.

How long had Deputy Hay been in the next room? Had he overheard their conversation? Damn Fiona! She noticed I was wearing the charm yesterday and now I'm not. If they find it in Harry's room, I'll be the deputy's number one suspect, for sure.

How could she gain entrance? She looked outside and saw the maid's cart. Maids had a skeleton key that would let them into all the rooms. She grabbed the key, approached Harry's room, slipped under the crime scene tape, and closed the door behind her.

It was weird being in Harry's bedroom again. The body was gone. The harp was gone. The room smelled of chemicals, but if she tried hard enough, she could still distinguish the lingering trace of his scent. She opened the wardrobe and ran her hands over his suits, grabbed a sweater from the drawer, scrunched it with her hands, and buried her nose in it. There, that was better. That was Harry. She replayed what happened that night in her mind.

When she went to his room that evening, she wanted nothing more than to hear from Harry's lips that he was sorry for the pain he'd caused her. That he regretted shattering her dreams. That Fiona meant nothing to him. Instead, he'd told her, in a detached monotone that sounded like he'd memorized the spiel and used it a hundred times before, what they had was just a fling. Two adults on an erotic adventure. Fiona was right. Any woman would always play second fiddle to Terpsichore.

She'd implored Harry to give her another chance, but he asked her to leave before she embarrassed herself. She didn't care. She threw herself at him and declared her love again and again.

He laughed at her. Called her a sweet young thing. Told her to find someone her own age. Get married, settle down, have a passel of kids. Name one for him. Then he walked away and began to play his harp.

She hadn't meant to kill him but some monster she never knew was there came from deep within her. It pushed the harp toward Harry with one powerful, fateful thrust. She'd never forget the surprised look on his face as he grabbed at her. That must have been when she lost the charm. That is when she'd lost the good part of her.

Damn it! Where is it? She knelt on her hands and knees and searched, but no luck. "Well, if I can't find it, maybe they won't find it either," she said. She got up, brushed her pants off, walked to the door, and peered through the peephole. The coast was clear. She opened the door.

Deputy Hay was lying in wait for her. He held out his fist. "Fiona told me you might be looking for this." He opened his fist. Her charm lay on his palm. "The coroner's office found it grasped in Hannigan's hand. Millie Mason, I'm arresting you for the murder of Harry Hannigan."

What's Love Got to do With It?
Karen Keeley

Truth be told, we all felt pistol-whipped, the maestro's unrelenting quest for excellence driving us mad, forty musicians employed with a fledgling orchestra seeking to make inroads into the Vancouver arts scene. "Allegro!" he shouted. "You there," he pointed to single out Leonardo Giovanni on the cello. "I say again, allegro." He broke into Italian, imbecille, roditore, genio musicale non è!

"I am playing allegro," hollered Leo. "Her leg—bro." He pointed at Chelsea, she too, a graduate of the academy where most of us had learned our trade, although a couple of years behind Leonardo and me. "Whenever I go right, Chelsea goes left." Leo perched on the edge of his chair, back straight, cello clamped between his knees. "Why in heaven's name do you have us crammed in like herring in a fishbowl? It's impossible to work under these conditions."

There came the sound of an ambulance as it pulled into the back alley, siren blaring. The side door was propped open, hoping for air, hot as hell in the orchestra pit, the air-conditioning on the fritz. Whoever drove it neglected to kybosh the siren. The maestro covered his ears.

"Conditions!" he shouted. "I give you conditions! Vattene, vattene, begone." He stormed off, leaving us standing or sitting in our assigned spots, eyes wide with disbelief.

"That went well." Leonardo hollered over the noise of the siren which stopped, the sound deafening by its absence. He grabbed his cello and departed.

I chased after. "You can be a real pest, you know that?" I wondered, why the siren? Had someone taken ill? I hoped it wasn't any of the maintenance crew there to fix the air-conditioners. We had a concert in less than six weeks. If we didn't get our act together as an ensemble, we were toast.

Toast included Leo burning up the sidewalk. Despite his size, he could move like a linebacker when the mood hit him. He was late for a very important date, the reason he'd goaded the maestro into another temper tantrum. But if he lost this gig—a paying job—he'd flounder without a lifejacket, up the proverbial creek.

As an ensemble, we'd practised Beethoven's Fifth for weeks, the allegros, the andantes, and all the other gros and fortissimos which encapsulated the drama of the piece, a sense of imprisonment, followed by loss and conflict. Leo too, was conflicted, downright insufferable.

As he weaved through the crowd, bumped elbows with theatre goers and others intent on keeping their late-night dinner reservations, I struggled to keep up. It being a Thursday, Rosa would be singing at the Stardust, a well-known nightclub on E. Hastings. Think the Carpenters, Rosa's voice too, a silky contralto. Leo played the piano. It was for them I planned to commit murder. First, I had to dangle the bait—hook, line, and sinker.

To do that, I dropped my wallet, my comb, my sheet music throughout the following week, a move which allowed me to seductively bend at the waist, show off my ample cleavage, my silk blouse partially unbuttoned. The pencil-thin skirt and six-inch heels highlighted the length of my legs. I was nothing if not persistent. My persistence paid off.

* * *

I reserved a room under a false name at the Copper Queen Hotel near the waterfront on Powell, an establishment of questionable character, much like me. On any given night, only the down-and-out or the out-of-towners frequented the place, either because they were duped by an Uber driver after being picked up at the airport or they'd booked online, trusted the internet with their reservation, not realizing their mistake until after the damage was done.

The maestro arrived with a bottle of Chianti, fine by me. It meant we'd save the two bottles I brought for later, the Illuminati Ilico. I'd chosen that brand because of the name. Didn't Illuminati have something to do with religion? Something hinky? What I hadn't counted on was the sex—good sex, sex to die for.

Ever tried to make love while wearing earbuds? It was tricky but the maestro and I both got a kick out of it, listening to Beethoven's Fifth, loud and proud. For a little guy, he was good with his hands, his lips, his hips, and just about every other organ he'd honed to perfection. He played me like a piano, running his fingertips up and down my spine.

During our love making, I rode the wave, the music combined with the sex. The maestro kissed me, fondled my breasts, touched me in ways I'd never experienced. There was a flurry of butterfly kisses over my skin and before I knew it, I was moist and hot, and him throbbing to the tempo of Beethoven's Fifth, da da da dum, electrical currents coursed through both of our bodies.

When he entered me, I climaxed and by then I was past caring. I would've sold my grandmother to keep this party rolling. I groaned, "Holy mother," and the maestro smiled, a sweet smile—nothing like the snarling panther he could be when he tried to get the best out of us. We lay together, our breath coming fast, a feeling of emptiness I couldn't have explained and yet warm and fuzzy, too. Too bad it had to end.

I left the bed, pulled the top sheet with me. He lay there naked—the Greek god of love, Eros, Greek mythology another passion of mine. The maestro, older than me by a good many years, proved a healthy libido didn't come with an expiration date. He was clean-shaven with an exquisite aquiline nose, sensuous lips, and dark curly hair as wild and tangled as any of the greats, the kind of guy who left me weak in the knees.

"La mia dolcezza," he cooed, my sweetness. "Come back to bed. The night is young."

I stood by the window, the sheet wound around me. I turned, smiled, and held out a hand. He left the bed, came to me, and we wrapped up tight together, while overhead a gazillion stars and one full moon shone bright, its reflection shimmering on the dark waters that gave Vancouver harbour its name.

"Why are you here?" I asked.

"Mia cara—you invited me, did you not?"

He nibbled on an earlobe, gently blew into my ear. I felt a quiver in my midsection, a flutter that said, show me more. "You could've declined," I whispered.

"That would prove me a rude and heartless brute," he countered. "I am none of those things." His lips worked their way down the side of my neck, his hands explored, my mind ready to take flight on a wing and a prayer. I truly felt weak in the knees.

"There are those in the orchestra who say you are exactly those things," I told him.

He jerked away from me. "Who would say such a thing?"

He wanted to know more, who would dishonour his name, his character, question his impeccable commitment to the music—it was always about the music.

"It's just hearsay," I said. "Ugly rumours, ugly gossip. I shouldn't have mentioned it. Tonight is special, like you, like us."

We were on the sixth floor, nothing above us but a graveled roof. I looked down at the traffic below as it snaked along Powell, headlights and taillights, and traffic signals flashing amber.

I led him back to bed. We made love without the earbuds, slow, methodical, exploring each other in ways that defied explanation, letting nothing slip by, slip past, slip away, the velvet touch of my skin, his skin, both of us slippery with sweat, blood coursing. I tied his wrists to the bedframe, something he found both amusing and endearing. He trusted me. I was now in charge.

I moved slowly, used my hands and my tongue, and he soon had an erection. He moaned for release as I covered his body in butterfly kisses. I whispered, "Not yet, my love. Feel the agony, the ecstasy," but I don't think he heard me. His hips gyrated beneath me, his eyes rolled back in his head, the look of a trapped animal begging for release.

When I straddled his hips and he entered me, we climaxed together, the intense wave washing over the two of us like a tsunami. I thought I heard him whimper, almost a cry like a wounded kitten. It surprised me when I noticed tears in his eyes, never believing I could've been that good when I'd always prided myself on being very, very bad. I knew then, if this was original sin, count me in—hook, line, and sinker. Sadly, into each life a little rain must fall. In the maestro's case, it would be a deluge, a kind of last rites drowning in carnal pleasures, the least I could offer, considering what was to come.

* * *

Monday morning the police arrived at the theatre, our home away from home built in the thirties, a time when moviegoers flocked to the downtown East side in search of a diversion from their miserable lives. The men in blue brought with them the terrible news, the maestro was dead, his body discovered in a dumpster behind a sleazy hotel near the waterfront.

"Found this," said the lead investigator, a Detective Constable Torrance. He held out an earring sealed within an evidence bag.

"What is it?" asked Leonardo. He removed his horn-rimmed glasses and squinted at the bag. He thought the glasses made him look like Buddy Holly.

"An earring, quite distinct, found in the bed sheets," said the detective. "From the look of the place, he and his lady pal had a rockin' good time before she ended it, with him, I mean."

I rolled my eyes. "Rather unorthodox, wouldn't you say? Waving around a piece of evidence. Who's to stop whoever owns it from running home and tossing the mate?"

"Jewellery stores," said Torrance. "We're making the rounds, asking jewellers if they sold a pair like this one. We'll get the name."

"You think whoever was with him, killed him?" I asked.

"Seems likely." Torrance jabbed the bag under my nose. "Ever seen this before? Would it be yours by any chance? Save us the legwork."

I took a step back, to distance myself. "Not my job," I said. "Besides,

I've never seen it before." And I hadn't. I had no idea who owned the earring. Maybe the hotel staff lacked initiative when it came to cleaning the room and providing clean sheets. Leonardo looked at me sideways, ready to blurt out the inconceivable. He knew my love of jewellery. I had oodles of the stuff, some genuine, some costume, all gifts from previous lovers.

I leaned sideways, pretended to faint, and stepped down hard on his instep, made him holler. "Sorry," I mumbled. "I'm lightheaded, the sad news, our poor maestro dead."

"You didn't even like the guy." Leonardo rubbed his injured foot. "None of us did, pompous prick."

"It was like that, was it?" Torrance handed off the evidence bag to one of his colleagues. "Lots of suspects in this here group?"

"By this here group, if you mean the chamber orchestra, then yes," I told him. "We're approximately forty members from all walks of life. We work together, breathe together, come together as one."

Most of us were in attendance. Some stood against the back wall, used a tissue to dab at crocodile tears, others with little interest in Torrance's questions. "That's a lot of suspects." He frowned.

"Half are women, so yes. A lot of suspects," I echoed. "We practise five days a week which doesn't leave much time for anything else."

Those around me nodded in agreement, guilt evidenced by that little V between their eyes, proof of worry or concern over some past indiscretion. All except Chelsea. She was busy tearing the wrapper from a Mars Bar. She caught my look and mumbled, "Sorry, no breakfast." I shrugged. No skin off my nose, chocolate best left to the experts.

I told Torrance, "If you think it was one of us, I suggest you gather your facts before swinging your big stick in our direction, looking to knock over a likely candidate."

"It's going to be like that, is it?" The detective was not a happy man, especially not on a Monday with a murder to solve.

"Like what?" I asked, ever the innocent.

"Confrontational," snarled Torrance. "I hoped we'd all get along like one big happy family."

"The only family I have are the members of this troupe," I conceded. "As for the maestro, he came on board a year ago. He's originally from Italy, as you probably know, by way of Hoboken and Schenectady." I'd heard rumours, some kind of scandal, money pilfered, an unfortunate death, a body found floating in the Mohawk River. I kept those thoughts to myself, who was I to go pointing fingers?

"We were lucky to get him," I added. "Perhaps someone from his past tracked him down and acted on a past vendetta. Some indiscretion none of us are aware of. We didn't socialize with the man."

The detective was having none of it, choosing me as his sparring partner. "It wasn't indiscretion what ended the guy's life," he growled. "We found empty wine bottles, prints smudged, an empty bottle of barbiturates, again, prints smudged. One of the hotel's drapes was half torn from the curtain rod, remnants of broken violin strings found in the trash, the guy strangled, eardrums punctured. That could've happened when he fell, landed in the dumpster. If it wasn't for some homeless guy, we might never have discovered the body."

Never? That seemed unlikely but when it came to a girl's point of view, I kept my mouth shut, thinking the detective was under the impression all murderers were stone-cold killers.

"Maybe it was an accident." Leonardo massaged his other foot. "A kinky sex game gone wrong." Leo's comment surprised me. Did he have personal experience in that regard? As for accidental death, I was grateful he'd nudged the detective in that direction but the man remained skeptical, certain the maestro's death was deliberate.

Meanwhile, the image of the maestro's swollen tongue protruding from that beautifully chiselled jaw, his head of dark curls dishevelled, broken blood vessels in both eyes, filled me with guilt but not enough to start talking.

Leonardo and Rosa needed stability. They were living a fairy tale, certain that a one night gig at the Stardust would rocket them to the top of the pop charts, make them instant celebrities. Leo had the credentials, the knowledge, the expertise, a true virtuoso with string instruments, woodwinds, the horns, and percussion. He might not know it yet, but Leo was perfectly suited to the job as maestro.

* * *

Friday evening after rehearsals, he relaxed in his recliner with the television muted, some program about the mating habits of sea turtles. I paced the living room in an attempt to keep my anger in check. "Whaddya mean you don't want the job?"

Rosa was in the kitchen putting the finishing touches on the fettuccine with clam sauce. She'd whipped up a batch of bruschetta, an Italian loaf slit down the middle lengthwise and smothered in chopped fresh tomatoes, basil and black olives, all toasted to perfection. I knew then why Leonardo had married the gal—her people emigrated from northern Italy about a thousand years ago, some region called Trentino-Alto Adige or maybe it had been Veneto, where naturally blonde, blue-eyed women were prevalent, known for their beauty, charisma, and culinary delights.

"Rosa and me, we're gonna try and make it with the contemporary music scene," said Leo. "The owner at the Stardust offered us three nights a week, with an extension clause, if we keep bringing in the punters. Business has never been so good."

I plopped on the couch, dejected. "You have no idea, do you?" I said.

"No idea, what?" Leo sat there, toyed with a lace doily, something Rosa must've made during her free time. Was there anything the woman couldn't do?

I found myself suddenly wondering about their sex life, especially now Rosa was pregnant, having just learned that bit of news when I arrived. Did that call for an increased appetite for pasta and whole grains? Sex wasn't something Leo and I ever discussed, not when our relationship had been akin to family, Leo the baby brother and me, the bossy older sister, according to him. It started in grade school when the older kids picked on Leo, tripped him up, stole his shoelaces, called him four-eyes. More times than I could count, I found him face down in the mud, his glasses broken. I knew even then, a gal needed to grow a backbone which I did, thumping the other kids, a take-away that boded me well over the years. I incorporated their nastiness into my daily life, operated with stealth and slight-of-hand, caught those nasty schoolyard bullies off guard. They never knew what hit 'em. Their lockers broken into; homework lost. Favourite ballcap gone missing. Notes passed around in class, all crafted by me and signed by them. I became a pro at forging their signatures. The things I got away with. But not with Leo, the little scallywag. He'd crawled into my heart, and there he stayed, even all these years later. He and Rosa. Family I'd never had.

Rosa called us to dinner. She handed me a chilled bottle of Perrier, the expectation we three would navigate this pregnancy together—no more red wine. Leo turned off the television and followed me into the kitchen. I helped myself to the fettuccine, handed the dish to Leo. He was busy telling me, he'd stay with the orchestra until a replacement was found for our dearly departed maestro. After that, he and Rosa would move on. "There's a record label out there somewhere with our name on it," he said, honing in on the bruschetta.

Did they even do that anymore? Record labels. I twirled my pasta with a fork, my appetite pretty much in the toilet no matter how wonderful everything smelled. I couldn't believe they would gamble with their future, not with a baby on the way.

"It's not all Spotify and YouTube videos," Leo assured me. "It's about filling the stadium." He shoved a healthy forkful of pasta into his mouth, took a drink of his Perrier. "People still go to concerts. That's where the money is. You've been there. We've all been there. Think of Garth Brooks. He packs the place."

Of course, he did. He was Garth Brooks. That kind of talent packed every venue they played, just like the other concerts we'd been to over the years—Bruce Springsteen, John Fogerty, Robbie Robertson, me sandwiched between Leo and Rosa with a bunch of stoners crowded around, testing my patience.

* * *

Tuesday, out of respect for the maestro's death, the managing director postponed the concert, told us the future of the orchestra was in jeopardy. We were none too pleased about that. Detective Constable Torrance too, was none too pleased, wanting to review the events leading up to the maestro's death. He asked me about the setup of the orchestra.

"The double bass plays an octave lower than the cello," I told him. "The cello plays an octave—eight notes—lower than the viola. The viola duplicates the violin's three lower strings but the fourth string is tuned another fifth lower than the lowest string on a violin. It plays harmony to the violin's melody."

He looked at me like I was speaking Greek in the Galápagos Islands, wondering if Darwin's theory of evolution by natural selection had truly turned the animals into cartoon caricatures of themselves or was it solely based on environmental conditions and isolation.

Then it dawned on me; I could be maestro! I had, after all, graduated top of my class at the music academy, right up there with Leonardo Giovanni, something I'd been proud of.

"Violins are the highest pitched of the string family," I added. "There are first violins and second violins. They play different parts of the musical score. Rosin the bow incorrectly—too much rosin and you create a cloud of dust, the sound harsh, scratchy, downright excruciating. Think scorched cats."

I had my violin with me, placed it under my chin and gave a demonstration.

"Jesus," whispered Torrance.

"Jesus has nothing to do with it. It's all in the wrist, the placement of the bow."

He pulled at his top lip, thinking. "So you're sayin' the maestro was killed by violin music. He didn't get himself killed by a violin string."

"It's virtually impossible to strangle someone with a violin string," I assured him. "The string would snap." I knew that from personal experience. Two attempts, and both ended with snapped strings, each string threatening to whack me in the face but thankfully, quick reflexes saved me, the reason I'd resorted to using the curtain cord—thank you baby Jesus for the depressing drapes hung in that sleazy hotel room.

"Violin strings, whether they're made from catgut, nylon, or steel, will break over time." I plucked at the strings on my violin. "If you're truly curious, violin strings are not really made from catgut—they're made from sheep intestines, stretched, dried and twisted."

Torrance was not impressed with my string knowledge. He frowned as he watched me walk away. He followed, grabbed my arm, forced me to stop dead in my tracks. "Okay, Einstein. If you think you're so smart, tell me what happened. How does someone kill with music?"

"Einstein isn't my forte," I told him. "I'm more of a Julie Andrews type of gal. Do-Re-Mi, playing the scales." Surely, he'd heard of the Sound of Music? Then again, it appeared not. My attempt at humour fell on deaf ears.

"I've been with the ensemble a year," I added. "Before that, I played with the Seattle Symphony in the States, and before that, I taught music at a high school in Marpole. I was there three years after graduating the music academy. Leo's resume is similar despite his hankering to be a pop star."

"Those facts I don't need," snarled Torrance. "Tell me how it was done."

"Someone put headphones on the victim," I said. "They cranked up the sound and it pretty much blasted his eardrums. You've heard about opera singers—how they can shatter wine glasses with their voices."

Torrance nodded, deeply distressed. He ran his fingers through his mop of tangled curls, something I was just now beginning to notice, that and his chin, masterful, chiseled from marble.

I told him, "There has to be a flaw in the crystal. And the pitch has to be a perfect match. Same principle here—shattered eardrums. The excruciating pain caused the poor man to prance around the room where he got caught up in the drapes, tanked up on barbiturates and booze. He strangled himself with a curtain cord, not a violin string.

While he's struggling with that, he topples out of the window."

"Christ," groaned Torrance. "It's like something out of the Keystone Kops." I left him there and entered the maestro's office. Like a belligerent puppy, he followed, pulled out the maestro's chair, sat at the maestro's desk. The room was dark, much of it in shadow, same as the hallway. Torrance shrugged out of his trench coat while flicking on a desk lamp, the light cutting into the doom 'n gloom. "If all of that happened like you said, who brought the headphones?"

"Did you ask the hotel if they provided such a thing? Maybe the headphones were on hand, meant for TV watching. It could have been an accident, the person playing the music too loud, didn't realize the volume was detrimental to the maestro's hearing. Despite his chosen profession, perhaps the maestro had extremely sensitive hearing. When the poor man went bonkers, that scared the bejesus out of whoever was in the room. They grabbed their pantyhose and high-tailed it out of there."

Torrance looked doubtful. "Do women even wear pantyhose anymore?" I didn't bother with an answer. He growled, "That's a lot of maybes which means maybe you know something about what took place."

"I'm simply giving you my theories," I said. "I like to solve puzzles."

"Death by misadventure." Torrance wasn't fond of that result. "The guy wasn't pistol whipped by some ticked off broad who hunted him down, a cougar on the prowl. His past didn't come back to haunt him."

I laid my violin on the desk, sat, and crossed my legs. I stopped short of batting eyelashes. Torrance may have gotten first dibs on the maestro's chair, but the chair—and the desk—would soon be mine, if everything went according to plan.

I looked him in the eye. "Far be it from me to change the subject," I said, "but are you fond of Italian wine? I'm partial to something called Illuminati Ilico."

"Same wine as what was found in the dead guy's room." Skepticism again clouded his face. "Sure, I'm game." He'd picked up a paperclip and fiddled with it like it would provide some kind of insight. "For a violinist, you can be real pushy. You know that, right?"

I smiled. "Comes from playing the violin. Attack and retreat."

I thought about the music, how the riffs and melodies could encapsulate the pitter-patter of raindrops, the burble of a babbling brook, the fury of an approaching thunderstorm. I told Torrance, "Think drive, determination, and repetition."

Torrance too, believed in drive and determination, stipulating police tactics also called for such strategies—gather the suspects and hammer at the accused until they caved under pressure.

* * *

At quitting time, the good detective found me in a deserted parking lot, the rain still teeming down and me without an umbrella. My vehicle, an ancient Merc Grand Marquis sat dead in the water, a flooded carburetor. Torrance lifted the hood and fiddled with something resembling a butterfly wheel. Soon the vehicle purred like a kitten. We went to dinner at the Old Spaghetti Factory in Gastown, both of us looking like drowned cats, but the staff didn't seem to mind, offering us a booth in a secluded corner.

After we'd eaten, Torrance followed me home where we polished off that bottle of wine. The detective reminded me of the maestro, a man willing to do battle to preserve a woman's virtue, nothing sexier than the perception of a damsel in distress—I too, could play the game.

We listened to Vivaldi's Four Seasons, another favourite of mine, renewal, life, twilight and death, climaxing during the final movement, the music moving right through us, no time to catch our breath. The good detective had good moves too, despite his language, not as colourful as the maestro's, not unless comparing me to a pistol counted as colourful.

Eventually, I was offered the job as maestro on an interim basis. The managing director said we'd give it a six-month trial period, after he too, fell for my wily ways. I'm devoted to keeping the orchestra intact, determined to make the job mine. When it comes to the sex, I get it where I can, always climaxing just before the finale. With regard to Leonardo and Rosa, they're on the road, happy as clams, the baby due any day. Leo says they're making hay while the sun shines. Of course, they are. After baby's arrival, Rosa will be singing, what's love got to do with it, she and Leo drowning in diapers. If they think they're going to make me godmother, they've got another think coming. I've never wielded a magic wand though I have been known to ride a broomstick now and again.

Ruby Wants to Watch
Joseph S. Walker

They say people find themselves in college. I found a big part of myself late one night, when my roommate, Della, and the guy she picked up at a party, either thought I was asleep or they were too buzzed to care.

The room was almost dark, except for a thin line of illumination under the door and the faint glow the curtains gathered from a streetlamp. I listened to whispered endearments and pleadings, heard the rustle of clothes dropped to the floor. In the scant light their bodies' soft outlines moved clumsily on the narrow dorm mattress. I could just make out Della, as she pushed the boy's head down and draped a leg across his shoulder. She held his hair and hissed urgent instructions. Her back arched and she cried out loud yes, there.

I bit my lip and slipped a hand into my panties, found myself wet.

The boy moved up Della's body. She rolled him onto his back and straddled him. She told me later it was her first time on top. It took her a few seconds to figure out the angle and how to lower herself onto him. When she did, she held still for a long moment before she let out a shuddering moan I felt all the way down my spine. I watched Della rock against the boy, watched his arms reach up for her breasts. By then I had both my hands between my legs and a corner of the pillow between my teeth to try to keep quiet. When I came, it was explosive, more intense than I'd ever felt before. My whole body clenched and let go, leaving me drained, and shaken, and with the knowledge I was a voyeur.

It was surprising because porn almost never did anything for me. Too often it's a parade of smooth, sweatless, hairless bodies, with more tattoos than a biker bar and less fat than a granola bar, working through scripted positions with all the spontaneity of an assembly line. Mannequins with no histories and no dreams, fucking and sucking in blandly anonymous rooms with sparse furnishings and no personal touches. If not for the inevitable huge dicks and erect nipples, it would be Ken and Barbie bumping against each other in the dream house, with about the same emotional charge. What got me going was people. Real people, with their body hair and blemishes, their flabby areas, their fumbles, their ecstatic moments of release. No porn star can convincingly mimic the emotions of somebody who wasn't expecting to get laid.

Maybe things would have been different if I weren't this way, or if Carmen hadn't gone to such lengths to indulge me.

Maybe I wouldn't wake up sometimes with the faces of two dead men hanging in the air in front of me.

* * *

I met Carmen eight years after college, well into my career as a financial planner. Carmen worked IT, and we had condos in the same high rise. Casual chats by the mailboxes turned into casual dinners at the place around the corner, then casual drinks at the bar across the street, and eventually kisses that didn't feel casual at all.

Carmen was willing to take things slow. I hadn't dated a woman since leaving school, and I had just broken up with a guy after I figured out he stole from me. I wondered how he was going to explain my name tattooed on his chest to future partners. Maybe he'd say Ruby was his mother or his birthstone. I didn't care, as long as he stayed away. I took my time, unsure how serious I was to be with anyone new.

One spring night we were in the park. There was still a hint of chill in the air, and not many people around. I held Carmen's hand and thought this might be the night I asked her back to my place. She nudged me. "You see that?" she asked. "That couple we just passed ducked into the woods."

I stopped dead and turned around, bringing Carmen up short. "Where?"

She pointed at a dense little thicket of trees. I pulled her off the path. "Let's see what they're doing."

"Bet I already know," Carmen said, but she followed. We moved into the trees as silently as we could. In a couple of minutes, I spotted them in a small clearing. The full moon gave more than enough light to see the man backed against a tree. He had one hand above his head, holding a small branch, and the other tangled in the hair of the woman crouched in front of him, sucking his cock.

I pulled Carmen to where we could see through a narrow gap between trees. My breath got shallow. I pushed myself back against Carmen and she wrapped her arms around me from behind. I put my hands on hers and moved them up to my breasts, smiled at her little start of surprise. I watched the man against the tree, the way his face twisted, and his chest heaved. I put a hand back and pushed it against Carmen's groin and she ground against it.

The woman broke away. She took off her jacket, spread it on the ground, reclined on it, pulled her skirt up to her waist. The man knelt between her feet. She raised her legs and he pulled off her underwear, putting it to his face before he shoved it in a pocket and dropped his jeans to his knees. He put the woman's legs on his shoulders and reached down between their bodies. I could see it on his face, the moment he entered her.

Carmen undid my pants and they dropped to my ankles. I pressed my bare skin up against her, bending forward. I watched the couple fuck and tried to stay quiet as Carmen's hand explored me. One of her fingers slipped into me and withdrew and came back, joined by another. I bit my arm as she matched the rhythm of the couple in front of us.

* * *

Carmen did come home with me that night. I told her the story about Della while she undressed me and then herself. Her body was slender, boyish, and eager, and the way it fit against mine made me wish I hadn't wasted time being casual. Within a few weeks, she was essentially living

103

with me.

Carmen was funny, smart, cheerful, and endlessly fascinated by my need to watch. We took frequent late night walks in the park. We were rarely as lucky as that first night, but just being out together was exciting. She liked to sit on the couch and pretend I wasn't in the room as she stripped and ran her hands over herself. I watched for the quiver of her stomach that meant her excitement had overtaken her self-consciousness. When she closed her eyes and put her hand to her pussy, I would get as close as possible, kneeling on the floor where I could watch the muscles shifting under her skin, listen to her breathing grow ragged, feel the warmth of her in the air.

We'd been together almost a year when I came home from work on Valentine's Day with a bouquet of two dozen roses, the kind of cheesy thing I did as a joke that wasn't really a joke.

"I've got something for you, too," Carmen said, eyes shining. She led me into the living room and sat with me on the couch, facing the big TV. She hit keys on her laptop and the TV came alive, to show a neatly arranged living room. It took me a beat to realize it was her condo, two floors below us. I looked at her, confused. She winked, nodded at the screen, and hit more keys. The view changed to her kitchen, her entry hallway, the shower, and finally several different angles on her bed. All the shots were clear and detailed and focused. She hit one final key and the TV split into twelve smaller windows, to show all the views.

"Well, I can see you've cleaned the place," I said. "But I don't get it."

"Hidden cameras," Carmen said. "One's in a phony smoke detector, one's in a teddy bear propped on a shelf. You get the idea."

"Okay. Still not getting it."

She turned to face me, crossed her legs. "Have you heard of an app called Just A Room?"

"Nope."

"It's like the ones where people rent out their places as vacation homes, except this one charges by the hour. All the advertising is about rent a room, take a nap or work on a project where it's quiet or just meditate, but that's a joke. What do you think is the main reason somebody might feel a sudden, pressing need for a room with a bed for just a little while, without the hassle of a hotel?"

Light dawned. I looked back at the TV. "Oh, my."

She put the laptop aside and scooted closer, wrapped her legs around me from the side, and put her mouth close to my ear. "The cameras are motion activated and everything is saved to my drives up here, so if somebody uses it during the day, we can watch when we get home at night, here or in the bedroom. We get sound, too."

My face felt warm as I stared. "Is this legal?"

Carmen kissed the side of my neck. "Do you care?"

* * *

At first, it seemed like it was going to be a bust. It was three days before we came home to the blinking light that meant the cameras had been active. We started the recording and watched as a stocky man in an expensive suit stripped to his underwear, got into the bed, and took a nap.

I laughed as Carmen fast forwarded. "Son of a bitch could at least jack off," she muttered.

Our next customer was a woman in her seventies. She plugged in five cell phones and spent three hours picking them up, one after another, having shouted conversations in what sounded like Russian.

"Maybe she's having phone sex," I said, to get Carmen over her frustration.

"I don't want to meet anyone aroused by that voice," she said. "Sounds about as erotic as a dental drill. Where the hell are all the horny people in this town?"

We found out a few days later. Afraid of another disappointment, we didn't watch the third visitor until after dinner, when we were propped up in bed with a couple of glasses of wine.

This man was tall and solidly built, with close-cut black hair going gray at the temples. He carried a cello case. Our building was just a block away from one of the city's big orchestra halls, so it wasn't unusual to see people with instruments on the streets. Carmen laughed. "Check out Mister Music," she said. The man took the case into the living room, set it on the coffee table, and opened it. Sitting on the couch, he put the cello between his legs, adjusted the strings, and began to play.

"Terrific," Carmen said. "Now we have a rehearsal hall."

"Beats screaming in Russian." I took a sip from my glass. "He's pretty good."

Carmen reached for her laptop to fast forward when there was a knock. Mr. Music shifted the cello aside and went to the front door, let in a red-headed woman with a violin case. "Sorry," she said. The sound was tinny but clear. "He was a fucking asshole today, kept making us go over that fourth movement. How much time have you got?"

Mr. Music looked at his watch. "Little over an hour."

"Well, then." The redhead kissed him. "We'd better get to it."

Carmen pumped her fist. "Finally!"

Mr. Music and the redhead moved into Carmen's bedroom. I had been in that bed. I had been naked in that bed. There was a tingle at the back of my neck as they fell across it. They kissed for several minutes before Mr. Music stood and began to take off his clothes. The redhead rolled off the other side of the bed and the two of them grinned and watched each other strip. I reached for Carmen's hand. She took mine and brought it to her mouth and sucked the tip of my index finger.

"Pause it," I said a few minutes later. I could hear the huskiness in my voice. We stared at the screen. The redhead was on her hands and knees in the middle of the bed and Mr. Music was behind her, his hand on her hips, to hold her in place as he fucked her. The need built from the pit of my stomach. I began to take my clothes off. My legs trembled. "Do that to me," I said. "Do that to me while we watch. Please." Carmen opened the bedside table for the strap-on while I imitated the woman's position as closely as I could.

Carmen began the playback again before she began to touch me.

* * *

It was a week before Mr. Music returned. We had one customer in the meantime, a woman in her early twenties who brought a man several years older. We pieced together from their conversation he had been her professor the previous semester, and she developed a crush on him. She reminded him she was no longer his student, but he was so nervous about being fired he couldn't get hard until she'd spent an hour handling him while whispering so softly in his ear we couldn't hear. It wasn't as arousing as Mr. Music's session, but as a soap opera it was highly diverting.

On his second visit, Mr. Music once again played cello in Carmen's living room as he waited. This time it was about twenty minutes before the knock. Instead of the redhead, a blonde, six inches shorter and perhaps thirty pounds heavier, came in.

I was propped up between Carmen's legs on the bed as we watched the blonde melt into Mr. Music's embrace. "Well, well," Carmen said. She stroked my side with gentle brushes of her fingertips. "Our boy is popular."

Mr. Music led the blonde into the bedroom and sat on the bed, still fully clothed. The blonde laid across his lap and he flipped her skirt up. Carmen switched angles so we could see her bared ass as he began to spank it. The percussive noise of the first hard blow made us both jump. After the twelfth, with his bright red handprint visible on both cheeks, he put his hand between her legs and pushed three fingers into her and the woman screamed and then choked out a strained thank you, sir.

"Ever been spanked?" Carmen breathed in my ear.

"Not like that," I said. "But I think I'm about to." I rolled onto my stomach and draped myself across her. "Don't be gentle."

* * *

Two days later Mr. Music opened Carmen's door to a bald woman with an elaborate dragon tattoo on the side of her head. She had a saxophone case. The second she was inside, she handed him a pair of handcuffs. Mr. Music tossed the woman over his shoulder and carried her, laughing, into the bedroom. He threw her onto the mattress and used the cuffs to attach her to the headboard.

"We don't have handcuffs," Carmen said in a raspy voice. "We have duct tape."

"Go get it," I said. "Hurry."

* * *

We did watch other visitors as the weeks passed, some worthy of being saved to Carmen's permanent archive. She always saved Mr. Music's sessions. He showed up at least once a week, often more. Always in the middle of the afternoon, always playing his cello while he waited for his partner of the day. We saw him with six different women, and we got in the habit of trying to guess which would turn up.

"The blonde," Carmen said one night in July as she started the latest recording.

"Dragon lady," I countered. We'd bought handcuffs since her last visit. I was hoping to try them out.

Mr. Music opened the door, and a man came in. Carmen and I looked at each other, eyebrows raised. The newcomer had thin brown hair and a neatly trimmed beard. Mr. Music pushed him up against the wall and kissed him for a long minute before breaking away. "You ready?"

"Yes," the man said.

"Yes, what?" Mr. Music asked.

"Yes, sir. Please."

Mr. Music went into the bedroom. He dropped his clothes in a pile and stretched out in the middle of the mattress, his legs spread and his fingers laced behind his head. The new man took his clothes off. His body was hairy, with a slight paunch, and he was enormously erect. He crawled onto the bed between Mr. Music's legs and took him in his mouth.

* * *

For Carmen's birthday in September, I got us tickets to see the orchestra. I bought a red dress. Carmen wore a tuxedo. I talked her out of the top hat.

When the orchestra came on stage, it was shocking to see Mr. Music in real life, without the intervening camera and screen. I knew every inch of his body, but with his formal wear and serious expression he seemed a stranger—which, of course, he was. Within a few minutes, we spotted all six of his women, nudging each other and trying not to laugh. The music was superb, but it was hard to listen as I looked between them. They all appeared professional and collected, like anybody else you might see in the course of a day. I glanced around at the audience, privileged and polished and poised, and wanted to know them all just the way I had come to know him. I wanted to see them all in the moments when they were fevered in desire, know the secret silent selves they revealed only when they had their hands on someone's skin. I shifted in my seat and tried to focus on the melody.

At intermission we consulted the program, which included headshots along with the names and biographies of the musicians. Mr. Music was Benjamin Snyder, first chair cello. The biographies of three of the women we'd seen him with said they were married.

"I don't see the beard," I said. I flipped through the book again, thought perhaps he was just out sick.

"Just spotted him," Carmen said. "He's in the audience. First box on the right."

It was a private box for two. The man we'd watched with Snyder sat next to a woman who might have been a couple of years older. Both were absorbed in their phones.

Carmen went up the aisle and talked to an usher. She was back in a few minutes, taking her phone from her pocket. Her thumbs sped across the screen. "Woman is Katerina Magnusson," she said. "One of the orchestra's most generous donors, the guy said. The beard is her husband, John. I'm Googling—" Carmen broke off, stared at the screen. "Christ." She dropped her voice. "Her father is Boris Lebedev."

"You're kidding." I glanced back at the box. Boris Lebedev was one of the city's best-known gangsters or, as his lawyers would have insisted, alleged gangsters. Just a few months ago, he had beaten a money laundering charge in a widely covered trial. "You think Mr. Music knows?" Before Carmen could answer, the lights dimmed and the musicians came back on stage. By the time the concert ended, we'd both forgotten about Lebedev.

* * *

It was a Thursday about a month later when we got home to the familiar flashing light. We'd met for drinks after work, and we both felt loose and giggly. Carmen grabbed her laptop and flopped onto the couch. "Let's see who was in the matinee today," she said.

I kicked off my heels. "Serve me up something spicy, mama."

Carmen frowned. "This is weird. App says whoever rented the place today never closed out their session. They're still there, been there more than seven hours."

"Huh." I fell onto the couch beside her. "Let's look at a live shot."

Carmen hit keys and the wide shot of the bedroom came up. I heard Carmen give a half scream, muffled as she slapped a hand over her mouth. I stood without thinking, my mouth open. Mr. Music was on the bed, nude. Some kind of stick was protruding from the left side of his chest, and the front of his body and much of the bed was red with blood. His head was turned to the side, and his glassy eyes seemed to look right into the camera.

Carmen killed the screen and pushed the laptop to the floor. She leaned forward, hugged her knees and trembled violently. I put my arms around her, tried not to collapse, and we sat that way for a long time.

"He was dead, right?" she said.

"Yes," I said. "Yes, baby, he was dead."

"What are we going to do?"

"I don't know. I don't know." I took a long breath. "Oh, god, Carmen. We have to watch the tape. We have to see who did it." I pushed myself erect. "I can do it alone. You don't need to watch."

"No." She took a long breath and reached for the laptop. "We'll do it together."

I sat as close to her as I could. She clutched my hand like a lifeline, working one-handed to get the day's recording up. She sped past Mr. Music's cello practice, returned to normal speed as he opened the door.

It was the beard who came in. John Magnusson.

As usual, the two men didn't say much to each other before they headed for the bedroom. If they did what they did the other three times we'd watched them, Magnusson was going to give Mr. Music—no, I reminded myself, Benjamin Snyder—two blowjobs, with a long interlude of cuddling in between, then jack off himself. "Fast forward," I said. The recording began to zip by, anything erotic in it now just grotesque. After Snyder came, Magnusson crawled up the bed and tucked himself under Snyder's arm. Usually, the two of them dozed a bit before Magnusson would play with Snyder's cock to get him ready for round two. This time, the timer in the corner of the screen said it had been about ten minutes when Magnusson abruptly stood, his face contorted.

"There," I said. "Rewind a little. Let's hear what they're saying." Carmen took us back about a minute and hit play.

"I'm not gonna argue," Snyder said. "Wendy deserves an honest effort."

Magnusson snorted. "Don't give me that. You know you can't stop."

Snyder shrugged. "Maybe not, but I'm going to try."

"So that's it? You decide to get married, and we're just done?" Magnusson rolled onto his back and crossed his arms. "I'm married. Half the whores I know you're screwing are married."

"I'm not responsible for your marriage. Or theirs. I will be for mine."

Magnusson shook his head. "You can't do this to me. You're all I've got."

"You've got Katerina. And Katerina's money."

Magnusson jumped from the bed and began to pace. I thought he was crying. "Asshole. You know that's not fair."

"You married for money," Snyder said. As Magnusson grew more agitated, Snyder got calmer. He seemed drowsy, and his eyes were closed. "I'm sorry money turns out to be a lousy lay."

"Fuck you. You know how hard I work to keep on that harpy bitch's good side."

"This is tiresome," Snyder said. He stretched and yawned. "It's not like you thought we were going to ride off into the sunset together. You just need a guy who's willing to get sucked and keep it quiet. Can't be that hard to find."

"You know I can't risk it." Magnusson sat on the edge of the bed and put his hand on Snyder's thigh. "I love you."

Snyder laughed. I wish he hadn't laughed. "Go home, John. Try to have some trace of dignity."

Magnusson stormed out. Carmen switched cameras to follow him. He went into the living room and stared out the window, still naked. He was still so long that I was about to ask Carmen if she'd paused. Abruptly, he turned. He walked to Snyder's open cello case and grabbed something from a compartment inside the lid. We learned later it was an endpin, the solid support the instrument rests on while being played. The bottom of the shaft comes to a sharp point to bite into the floor and hold it steady for the musician. A lot of people put rubber caps on them to protect the flooring.

Benjamin Snyder liked his endpins sharp.

Magnusson walked back into the bedroom, where Mr. Music was still on his back. He looked asleep. I hoped he was asleep. Magnusson never broke stride. He brought the endpin around with all the force he could muster and drove it into his lover's chest.

* * *

We took a long, mostly silent break before we fast forwarded through the rest. Magnusson spent a long time on the floor beside the bed, beating his fists against the carpet. At last, he stood. He took a long shower to rid himself of Snyder's blood. He dressed, found cleaning supplies and wiped down anything he might have touched. It was almost two hours before he left, taking Snyder's cell phone with him.

Carmen turned the TV off and we stared at our reflections in the blank screen.

"We can't show this to the police," she said. "We'd probably both go to jail. Get ourselves on the sex offender registry. For sure we'd both lose our jobs and they'd make sure I never touch a computer again."

"I know," I said. "But we owe him something. We can't let Magnusson get away with it."

"He won't. He cleaned up, but they'll find something. DNA. Clues."

"Clues," I said.

"They'll find something. Or somebody will tell them something." She stood. "I have to go find him." She visited the condo after every time it was used to clean and straighten, one of the requirements of using the app.

"I'm not letting you do that alone." I took her hand. "We'll go down together. I'm sure you're right. They'll find something."

* * *

They didn't.

The murder of one of the city's most prominent classical musicians was front page news, which meant enormous pressure on the police to make an arrest. Since Snyder had always been the one to make reservations, there was no record of who he had been with. Carmen and I told the police the app was just a way for us to make spending money from the spare condo after we moved in together. We didn't mention the cameras, and the ones Carmen hadn't been able to remove were not found.

The investigation turned up four of the women Snyder had brought to the condo. Each was interviewed and released, though not without being subjected to a storm of media coverage. As the list of Snyder's conquests grew, Twitter filled with jokes about classical music being a secret realm of sexual indulgence. None of it seemed amusing to me as the days dragged on without an arrest.

Snyder had been dead more than two weeks when I scrolled through the webpages of both city newspapers and couldn't find a single story about the investigation. "This isn't working," I said. "They can't keep on this forever. If they were going to find Magnusson, they would have by now."

"I know," Carmen said. She ran a hand through her hair. "I keep thinking about an anonymous tip, but I read they've gotten hundreds. Without other evidence it's no good."

I put my tablet down. "I have another idea," I said.

* * *

We were slow and careful, broke it down to be sure it couldn't be traced to us. We bought the envelope and flash drive from separate office supply stores and paid cash. Carmen bought a used laptop at a pawnshop, scrubbed it of information, and used it to put the movie she'd edited on the flash drive. It started with multiple instances of Magnusson going down on Snyder, followed by the conversation, where he called his wife a harpy bitch and admitted he'd married her for money. Then, the murder.

We alternated when we wrote the address on the envelope one letter at a time, used our left hands. The hard part was to find an address to use, since reputed mob bosses don't go out of their way to share details of their personal lives, but Carmen had done some work for the state revenue department and could still access tax records. We added personal and private after Boris Lebedev.

Five days later, John Magnusson was found in an alley with two bullets in his head.

* * *

I hope they made it fast and easy for him. I understood how he got to the place he got to, because I know the enormity of getting what you need, finding the thing that speaks to the urgency inside you, the sizzling electric pulse that connects mind and gut and groin. Knowing what it's like to have makes it possible to imagine what it must be like to have it snatched away. I tell myself Carmen and I did nothing wrong. If we hadn't watched, Ben Snyder would have still had his adventures. John Magnusson still would have killed him. We made sure he didn't get away with it. I don't find it convincing. Maybe, like science says, we changed things because we observed them. Maybe there are reasons some things happen behind closed doors.

It's been months since Magnusson died. Carmen and I haven't put the condo back on the app, though we did replace the bed. We haven't watched the old recordings, or even taken a late night walk in the park. But at lunch today, I found myself watch a couple at a table across the restaurant. I wondered what they looked like alone, together, and naked, what secret silent parts of themselves would be exposed. I felt something like the old tingle. I think tonight I will ask Carmen to pretend I'm not in the room. I'll ask her to touch herself, to let me see her taking herself to that place.

God help me, I still want to watch.

The Cello of Monkey Pawn Shop
Linda Kay Hardie

I found the cello when I was walking downtown in late May 2022. Reno's city center was full of tall casinos, grimy liquor stores, and brightly lit pawn shops, but also a veritable feast of restaurants. Casino restaurants were wonderful, created by classy second-tier chefs (the top chefs went to Las Vegas to open ultra-expensive and spectacularly brilliant eateries), while the street-level restaurants outside the casinos tended to be mom & pop shops, many of them Asian. Rents were lower than in the suburban parts of town.

I carried my wallet in a fanny pack strapped tight around my ample waist. In my jeans pocket, I had half a dozen five-dollar bills to hand out to the mendicants. As a single woman, I was often told to be afraid to walk downtown because of the so-called "bums." My friend Jack taught me awareness, compassion, and generosity. He was homeless for about ten years before he got into "the system," and received housing and disability payments to keep him off the streets. Most important of all, he got mental illness medications and counseling from Northern Nevada Mental Health on Galletti Way.

Jack carved money out of his slim budget to share. He often walked the footpath along the river where homeless people lived and handed out five-dollar bills to anyone who asked for money.

"Sure, they may use it to buy liquor," he said. "Most are mentally ill and are self-medicating. Whatever it takes to get you through the night."

Now Jack was long gone, dead from an accident in his home, and I was on the lookout for another good friend to share Reno's restaurants. I'm not a very convivial person and finding friends has always been hard for me. In the meantime, I refuse to miss out on good food. I was headed to a small, hole-in-the-wall bibimbap place to lunch alone when I passed a slightly grubby-looking pawn shop on a side street. Anyone who knows Reno would've been intrigued, too. Reno's pawn business was aboveboard, clean, and well-lit. Kind of boring. The shops were across well-lit streets from the casinos. There were other pawn stores, at the edge of business districts, just as clean and bright.

This one had a small, hand-painted sign in the window to declare itself Monkey Pawn. But instead of electronics and jewelry in the front window, I saw items that would be more at home in a Middle Eastern bazaar. Small- and medium-sized items, like statues of goddesses from cultures around the world and through the ages. Bric-a-brac gold-trimmed tea sets, and porcelain pussycats with mysterious gazes. Yes, even a lamp Aladdin would be proud to own.

Rather than the expected electronic buzzer, a bell tinkled when I stepped through the door. To my right I saw full bookshelves. Books in a pawn shop? I had definitely fallen down a rabbit hole. Curiouser and curiouser, my mind quoted.

The books were vintage. No paperback airport thrillers, these were hardbacks without dust jackets. And eclectic. *A Girl of the Limberlost* was one title I recognized. I had that book, a hundred-year-old edition, at home. This looked identical. There seemed to be no rhyme or reason to the shelving, with a first edition illustrated Junior Library of my heroine's adventures in Wonderland touching shoulders with an *Encyclopedic Cookbook* by the Culinary Arts Institute from 1948.

A Beginner's Guide to the Cello, a cloth-bound book with gold lettering on the spine, was next. I'd always been fascinated by the sound, size, and shape of a cello. My parents refused to buy or rent any instrument for me, so I learned to play the piano mostly because the school had one. I was never very good since I couldn't practice at home but I felt a kinship with music. I flipped open the cover to see $13.95 lightly written in pencil. Hmm. Maybe.

There was nothing new in this pawn shop. The jewelry, in an old-fashioned glass case at the back of the store, was vintage as well as beautiful. Not gaudy, but Victorian and ornate. There were the usual pawn shop denizens: Musical instruments. I started toward them.

I hadn't noticed the proprietor until she spoke. "Attractive instrument, the cello."

I'd just seen it. A beautiful golden color, polished to a high gloss. I plucked a string. In tune, and well-cared-for through its many decades of life.

"Yes," I replied. "Does it sound as beautiful?"

The old woman—at least 20 years older than me, and I'm 57—picked up the instrument and drew its bow across the strings. The cello wept with pleasure to tell a narrative of pain and loss.

"Look at this." She turned the instrument around.

On the back, which looked as golden and well-kept as the rest, was a poem written in old-fashioned calligraphy:

Make three wishes

There's no return to sender.

You're also attractive

To your preferred gender.

My skepticism kicked in. The phrasing was awfully modern for such a distinguished antique. It intrigued me, but not as much as the instrument itself. While I now doubted its age, it did have a wonderful sound.

"How much?" I asked.

The proprietor flipped over a white card tied by a string to a peg on the cello to reveal $999. A little pricey, but not out of line for a decent cello. If this were as old as it first appeared, it would be a bargain.

A tax refund threatened to burn a hole in my debit card as a childhood fantasy bubbled through my head.

"Throw in the book about cellos." I pointed backward with my thumb toward the bookshelves by the door. "And you've got a deal."

She reached her hand across the counter. An old-fashioned handshake, in this day and age? Okay, but her electronic reader with familiar credit card logos was modern enough. Minutes later I walked back to my car, parked in a free parking zone nine blocks away, with a large black case in one hand and an old book in the other. So much for bibimbap today.

"Any loose change, ma'am?" A voice broke into my reverie. I stopped near the downtown McDonald's to see a bearded man with a large backpack. Probably a veteran. Too many of the homeless people were war vets.

I looked down at my hands. "Hold this." I handed him the cello case and reached into my pocket. "Is a bill okay?" I presented him with a fiver.

It was fine. He handed back my instrument and smiled.

"Thank you, ma'am!" he said, and headed into the fast-food joint.

At home, I admired the cello. It was gorgeous. As I ran my hands over its curves, I wished I could play well enough to do justice to this piece of art. I learned to play the cello freakishly fast, but at the time, it didn't seem strange. Skillful enough to play in public with a string quartet after only five weeks?

* * *

I met Stella in Wingfield Park on the Truckee River. It was Pride Day 2022, at Reno's July Artown event when we were able to do a real festival again after the worst of covid. She staffed a booth for a liberal candidate. When I came to her table, she recognized me from a performance with my quartet in the entertainment tent. We got to talking about her candidate and the upcoming election. Next thing we knew, her shift was over, and she asked if I'd like to visit the food trucks. I would. We talked until dark, didn't even notice the festival tents come down until one of the food truck proprietors asked if she could have her table back so she could leave.

After the Pride festival, we walked to the Arch Society, a dessert bar in Reno's Midtown. I had the lemon meringue martini, Stella had the lavender lemonade, an adult beverage. We shared the lemon lavender macarons, our hands touching as we reached for the cookies.

I've never had sex on the first date before, but this was different. It felt inevitable, like true love. We were too keyed up to walk to our cars, so we took an Uber straight to her condo on the river in the Dickerson art district. We tugged on each other's clothes as we closed the front door behind us, our mouths locked together.

"I don't have a lot of experience with women," I said when we made it to the bedroom. "Or any. I came out after menopause. I had strict parents. The thought of being a lesbian never entered my mind until I no longer had any fucks to give about what other people thought of me."

Stella laughed. "That's okay, Laura, my love. I'll be your guide."

And she was.

Stella kissed me, a long, deep kiss with tongue. She ran her fingers through my short hair. This I could do. I kissed her, too, and rubbed her shoulders. She stepped away, and pulled off her blouse, freeing breasts unbound by a bra.

"Lick them, suck them," Stella said. "You know you want to."

Yes, I did. I licked first the left nipple, then the right. I sucked that nipple into my mouth and rubbed my tongue over it, feeling it harden into a small knot. Stella moaned. I nibbled, and she gasped.

My cunt started to throb, and I moaned, too. I continued to suck her hard button until she pushed me away. "No, not too much," she said. "Not too quickly."

Stella pulled my T-shirt over my head. My tits were restricted in a sports bra, much more comfortable than a regular bra. I no longer cared whether my breasts looked perky for men and a sports bra held them in place. Stella nipped at my nips through the fabric, then pulled it off over my head. She pulled my left nipple into her mouth and tongued it. My knees turned to water, and it was my turn to moan.

Stella removed her mouth, took my hand, and led me to the bed. She unsnapped and unzipped my jeans, and pulled them, along with my panties, down to my ankles. She reached a finger into my wet cunt and circled my clit. My back arched, and I almost came, but she pulled her finger back.

"No, not yet," she murmured. "I want you to have the whole experience your first time. I want to pop your lez cherry."

"Please," I begged. "Oh, please. Do whatever you want to me."

"I will."

"Then I want to suck your tits more and lick your cunt until you scream for me."

"Yes, my darling," she whispered.

I stepped out of my pants, and she eased me onto the bed, crawled between my legs, and sank her head into my bush. When her tongue circled my clit, I felt a warmth spread from my cunt, up to my heart, down my legs, out my arms, and up to my head, where it escaped through my mouth in a gasp.

"Oh, goddess!" I nearly growled as my back arched.

The waves crashed. And crashed and crashed. The orgasm was longer and deeper than I'd ever felt with a man. Stella's tongue licked and circled. I continued to burst into the cosmos. And then the crash, when I fell back to earth, and landed softly in Stella's arms. She left my cunt and moved up to kiss me again to keep me from screaming out my wonder.

"Oh," was all I could say. "Oh, my love."

She kissed my nose. "I'm so glad."

"Your turn," I said. And turned over to crawl down the bed.

"That's okay. It's your first time, I don't need ..."

"Yes. You do."

I was amazed how sensitive and responsive her little clit was when I put my tongue to it. It twitched, then hardened. I nibbled it. Stella stuffed her fist in her mouth to muffle a scream.

I lifted my head. "Ah." Then I did it again.

Before I knew I was queer, I thought I would never be able to lick a pussy, but now I felt it was a privilege to give as good as I got. I licked. Slow at first, then faster, then nipped again. Stella arched her back and made noises deep in her throat. Her body vibrated, then she collapsed into the covers. She sighed.

"Wow," she said. "And you've never done this before?"

"I have a good teacher."

In the morning, the sun sliced through the vertical blinds into her bedroom, Stella asked me how long I'd played the cello.

"Five weeks," I said with pride.

Her mouth dropped open. "Wow, that's quick," she said. "Did you already play the violin or some other instrument?"

"No, but I got a great beginner's book on how to play."

Over coffee and croissants, I gave her an abridged version of how I found the instrument, left out the part about the love poem on the back. I was embarrassed by that because it felt so tween-aged.

"That's charming," Stella smiled. "I wonder where it came from. Have you ever wanted to find out?"

We Ubered downtown to get our cars, then met at the main library a few blocks away, where we were able to park free because it was Sunday. Stella, an English professor experienced in research, found two other times the cello got involved in people's lives. Its antics undoubtedly went back much farther, but fifty years is as far back as we were able to trace with help from expert librarians.

We didn't do it in one afternoon. No, we spent a month, checked newspaper clipping files, old-fashioned microfiche files, thick reference books, and even old phone books. Those helped track down the surviving relatives of former cello owners. Eventually, we talked to them to get the kind of details the newspapers couldn't print.

Rather than present "just the facts" like Sergeant Joe Friday or the newspaper reporter I used to be, I decided to use Shahrazad's method and tell stories.

* * *

It was a seven-hour drive to Eugene for us in early September.

Pawn shops were not the ubiquitous places they were in Reno, especially not back in 1972. That's why relatives remember Clay found the cello in Monkey Pawn on his 21st birthday. He described it to his sister as "a quaint place with interesting old merchandise." Stella and I tracked Carole to a manufactured housing community, still on her own at age 76.

Carole told us, "He wasn't a musician, but he'd always wanted to be, so when he found the cello in late April for $175, he grabbed it, even though that was a month's rent."

Coincidentally, the shop also had a book for beginners on how to play the cello. The shopkeeper was mysterious about the instrument, pointed to a poem on the back, and that clinched the deal for Clay. All Carole could remember was it ended with "Makes you irresistible to women." I caught Stella shoot me a side-eye glance at that, but she didn't interrupt Carole.

Clay worked hard to learn to play, and amazingly he picked it up rather quickly. He advanced to where he could make musical sounds within several weeks, as opposed to his early squawks and screeches. Clay played actual songs out on his patio in the apartment complex. A woman heard him and peeked over the fence to see who the musician was. She was a pianist, and soon they were making beautiful music together in all sorts of ways.

Carole told us bluntly, "They fucked like rabbits," and said they once had loud sex in her bathroom during a big family Thanksgiving dinner. She was embarrassed. Her kids and their cousins, her sister's kids, were young and didn't know what the moans and thumps meant. Her husband gave her the eye and wanted to have their own "afternoon delight" in the master bathroom. Her sister and brother-in-law, evangelical Christians, blushed and tried to focus on their plates, while her elderly parents, who were going deaf, looked around, perplexed.

Clay and Alicia married before Christmas and honeymooned in Las Vegas, where they won a $100,000 jackpot. That would translate to more than half a million today. Alicia got pregnant right soon after. Her parents and Clay's were excited for a grandchild, especially a rich one.

Sounds like a happily ever after, doesn't it? But that's when things began going wrong.

"Clay must have taken the phrase on the back of the cello to heart because he couldn't keep it in his pants," Carole said. "Mostly with married women. Alicia found out and threatened to leave him, but it was too late. He'd cheated with the wrong woman, one with a psychotic husband."

The husband followed his wife one fall day to Clay's home. He burst in to find Alicia in a confrontation with the cheating couple. He went all Jack the

Ripper on them.

I imagine he yelled sexist slurs as he slit his wife's throat, then took the same knife to Clay and Alicia, slashed them to death in front of their baby daughter while everyone screamed. He left the little girl alone. Then he sat in the middle of the butchery and waited for the police because all the screams caused three sets of neighbors to call the cops.

Two of the officers vomited at the scene because of the gore and the fact the blood-soaked killer "looked like the devil himself," one of those officers told a reporter.

According to the newspapers, there was so much blood even professional crime scene cleaners couldn't get the room clean. The whole living room and dining room had to be stripped down to the studs and rebuilt. Management couldn't rent the apartment for five years. Legally, they didn't have to report the murder to prospective tenants, but neighbors were glad to gossip, and that cooled the market for that particular apartment.

The story was about to die down when it turned out Clay and Alicia didn't hit the jackpot in Vegas. Instead, Clay embezzled the funds from his job. There was no big estate for the daughter. She was put up for adoption. None of her family members wanted to raise the little no-longer-rich girl after what she'd seen. And what they'd seen.

The cello was one of only a few items in the room not damaged by the blood. Clay's sister sold the cello back to the pawn shop.

* * *

Stella and I drove to Fresno from Eugene, 11 hours straight, where the cello had turned up in 1997. We talked about the story we had heard. When we stopped for food at In-N-Out Burger in Medford, Oregon, I told her about the poem on the back of my cello. I'd forgotten about it until Carole mentioned a poem. It was strange the wording had changed. Or maybe it was just Clay's memory of how it went that was different.

Stella seemed subdued, but I didn't think much of it at the time, being rather stunned myself. I did ask her if she was okay, and she waved a dismissive hand. "I'm fine," she said.

* * *

Grubby-looking pawn shops like Monkey Pawn were not uncommon in Fresno 25 years ago, but Marianne had never seen this one before and found it strange that it didn't buy gold. That's what she told her friend Lindsey, whom we had tracked down from newspaper articles. But Marianne was drawn in by the tchotchkes in the window, just as I was. Like me, she talked to an old woman proprietor.

"It's hard to say how old the woman really was, since Marianne was 28, and everyone over 50 looked old to her," Lindsey told me with a laugh, being 53 herself by now.

Yet it wasn't a laughing matter. It started out well enough, just like for Clay. Marianne walked out of the pawn shop with the cello and the how-to book, having paid just under a month's rent. Lindsey remembered a poem on the back of the cello, something about wishes and being "tantalizing to the opposite sex."

"That last part I remember, because Marianne was in the middle of a dry spell in her love life. That promise appealed to her," Lindsey said. "It seemed to work, because she met Don within a month of buying that wretched instrument of hell."

"You blame the cello?" I asked. "You never said anything to the newspapers."

"Damn skippy I blame it," she said. "I would never say this to a reporter. I know it sounds crazy, but you'll understand. You've got the cursed thing, don't you?"

Stella and I looked at each other.

"If it were me, I'd burn the monstrosity," Lindsey said. "Throw it in a river. Take an ax to it. But I can see you're not going to do that. Just be careful."

Marianne had played the guitar in high school, but nothing orchestra-related. She learned to use the cello fast because she was obsessed with it, Lindsey said. She met Don when she answered a Craigslist ad for a cellist for a string quartet. Don played violin. They were sleeping together within a week and married six weeks later.

"But Marianne cheated on Don at their wedding," Lindsey said, shaking her head.

Marianne slept with the best man before the ceremony. Afterward, she was still in her wedding dress, going at it with the minister in a closet, when Don walked in on her.

"They had a full bar. Don's family had money and no expense was spared for their little boy," Lindsey said. "Don got roaring drunk, and he turned out to be a mean drunk." She shrugged. "Maybe he had a right to be, though."

Marianne rushed into the ballroom, rumpled from her tryst in the supply closet. The guests figured out what had been going on when the minister, also disheveled, appeared right behind her. The crowd stood around, drank a lot of wedding booze, and watched as the live soap opera unfolded in front of them.

"Marianne and Don had a screaming match in the middle of the ballroom," Lindsey said. "Don decked the minister, grabbed Marianne's arm, dragged her out to his car, which had been decorated by his buddies, and shoved her inside."

The newspaper printed a full-color photo of what the car looked like after the train hit it. There wasn't much of it left. You could see a white rose bud next to someone's severed arm on the ground. Lindsey was sure it was Marianne's. The accordioned car, which had been white, was painted red with blood.

"I still have the occasional nightmare," Lindsey said. She shuddered. "I don't know what got into her, because she never used to be like that."

The newspaper said both the newlyweds were decapitated when Don lost the race with the locomotive. The autopsy showed Marianne was six weeks pregnant. DNA established the baby wasn't Don's.

* * *

Stella and I were subdued as I drove us back to Reno, a five-hour drive. We stopped for gas in Stockton and Auburn and got sodas, but no snacks. We weren't hungry. When we got back to my house, we went right to bed. To sleep.

The next morning, while she brewed coffee, I retrieved the cello from my office at the other end of the house and showed Stella the verse on the back. She blanched.

"What is it?" I asked.

"I'm adopted," she said.

I nodded. She'd mentioned it. So?

"I never knew my birth family. They were a couple up in Eugene who were killed. My adoptive parents never made a mystery out of it, but they didn't give me any details. It wasn't until I applied for graduate school that I got curious and researched." She stopped to take a breath.

I needed another cup of coffee, so I motioned for her to wait a minute. I carried the cello with me to put it back in my office. Suddenly it made me very nervous.

When I returned with coffee, Stella told me a story about what looked like an idyllic marriage that ended with a triple homicide because her birth father cheated with a woman who had a vicious husband. The story expanded to include embezzlement that sullied this perfect union, too. One of her father's family mentioned a "cursed cello with a love spell" to the local newspaper.

"Are you thinking what I'm thinking?" Stella asked.

We sat in the sunny breakfast nook with our coffees. I gulped the last few mouthfuls of dark brew to avoid answering her for as long as possible.

"I hope not." I thought to save Stella's life, I would have to break up with her. Circumstances looked dire.

"Laura, be serious," she said. "Do you remember an old story called 'The Monkey's Paw'?"

I shook my head.

Stella looked around.

"What?" I asked.

"Where's the, you know, the c-e-l-l-o?"

"Why are you spelling?"

"Never mind. Where?"

"In my office."

"The other end of the house?"

"Yes," I said.

"It was a horror story from about 100 years ago," Stella began. "An old couple gets an enchanted mummified monkey's paw that can grant wishes, but with a twist. They wish for $200 to pay off their mortgage. Their son dies, and they get exactly $200 in death benefits. Two weeks after his funeral, the grieving wife persuaded the husband to wish for their son to come back. He did so, but he worried about what exactly would come back. When there was a knock at the door, he panicked and made his third wish. When his wife opened the door, no one was there but there was a rotten smell and some cemetery dirt."

"That's gross," I said. "What does that have to do with us?"

"What was the name of your pawn shop?" Stella said.

"Monkey Pawn... Oh."

"What did you wish when you got it?"

"First, I wished to be able to play it."

"Then?"

"To find true love." I reached out and held her hand.

"How did you phrase it?"

I thought for a moment. "I don't remember. I'm not sure I ever articulated it in a wish."

"Any other wishes?"

I concentrated. "I think one time when I was practicing, I said I wished I could know the story of the cello's history."

"Okay. Is that all?"

"Yes."

"Don't say anything remotely like a wish." Stella got up and headed to the back of the house. She returned moments later with the cello.

I opened my mouth, and she held up a warning finger. I closed it.

She held the cello by its neck and base and shook it. Nothing. She shook again, harder. The third time I heard a muffled clunk.

"I–"

Stella held up the finger again and I shut my trap again.

She shook the instrument more carefully.

"Reach into the f-hole," she said, holding the horizontal cello up a little.

I reached a finger in the curved hole. I nearly pulled it out when I felt something furry. I restrained myself and angled the thing to get it out of the hole.

"It's smaller than I thought," I said when it fell onto my other hand.

It was a mummified paw of some kind. Probably a monkey's.

"Outside," Stella said.

She led me out to my small backyard.

"Set it down there." She pointed to the middle of my small fire pit.

I set it in the center of the pit. Stella picked up three pieces of wood and tented them over the paw. I watched as she added crumpled newspaper and kindling, and then lit it. She was always good at making fires and soon had a roaring blaze.

I heard a high-pitched wail right at the edge of my ability to hear.

"What's that?" I said in a low tone.

"Probably the you-know-what," she said, in a whisper.

We sat down on our patio chairs and watched the fire, didn't speak. We sat for hours. Stella fed the fire. The sun was going down when the fire died down to coals. I felt something inside me snap like a twig.

"I don't think I know how to play the cello anymore," I said in a normal tone.

"That's okay," Stella said. "How do you feel about me?"

"I love you. I especially love you because you figured out how to save us from that thing."

Tears began to run down her cheeks. Oh, no! Had her feelings toward me changed?

"Honey?" I tried not to let my voice shake.

"I love you," she whispered. "I was afraid that spell would be broken, too, and you wouldn't love me anymore."

I started to cry. I stood and stepped in front of her chair. I took her hand and pulled her to her feet. "This morning, I tried to figure out how to break up with you so you wouldn't die from the curse." I stared into her eyes.

Stella sniffed, then chuckled. "We're not in the monkey paw story anymore. We're in an O. Henry story."

I laughed out loud. Only an English major!

Reed Between the Lines
Steve Liskow

Everyone in Chamberlaine County hated Grant Fuchs. It was hard to blame them.

Fuchs was the local art critic, and, the day after the Riverton Symphony's first outdoor concert of the summer, he wrote a review that took no prisoners and kicked the wounded. He tore the new conductor apart for his music selections. He gutted the soloists—both clarinetists—for their performance. The only favorable comment he made about the entire concert was that it ended.

The same night the review was published, someone beat Fuchs to death.

Two detectives visited me at my City Hall office the next day. I coordinated all the arts events for the town and I'd had my share of run-ins with Fuchs. I called him Grant Fuchs Everybody. Other people picked up on it.

"Grant was a wannabe everything," I said. "He couldn't paint, so he took it out on artists. He couldn't sing or play, so he picked on musicians. He was a lousy public speaker, so he gave actors and directors grief."

"Did he like anyone?" Winthrop had a profile that should have been on a coin. A flabby middle ruined the image. His partner, Symington, looked young and eager, sort of like a golden retriever puppy without a collar.

"Maybe his reflection."

"Tell us about the concert."

I tried not to quote the promo I posted on the town's website and sent to the paper.

"Our previous conductor died unexpectedly in spring of 2019. We had orchestra members fill in until we hired Stewart Crenshaw in September. The pandemic cancelled all the concerts in 2020, so Stew wanted to start this season with a bang. Lots of variety, lots of solos because he thought the musicians were good enough to deserve the spotlight."

"How did you select Crenshaw?"

"He got transferred from his job and settled in town in June of nineteen, heard about our need for a new conductor. He's got a music degree and plays piano, sax, and guitar. He's young, has good stage presence, and he gets along with people. He sounded like a perfect fit."

"So he had a lot at stake on this concert."

"We all did," I said. "Stew busted his ass to put the program together, but everyone else did, too."

I remembered when Stew told me he wanted to feature the two clarinetists, each for a different part of the program. Gina Bonadetta, who managed the local Apple store, was the soloist on Mozart's Clarinet Concerto, K. 622, which opened the evening. Danielle LaFreniere, who taught third grade, played clarinet for a medley of Benny Goodman swing classics. I wondered if Stew emphasized the reed players too much, but his enthusiasm was as contagious as poison ivy.

"Fuchs and Gina Bonadetta were divorced, weren't they?" Winthrop didn't make it a question.

I nodded. I'd been one of the men who consoled Gina after her breakup. She called marrying him the worst mistake of her life. We still dated sometimes. Actually, "dated" is a euphemism. Danielle and I knew each other in college, and I dated her, too. Same euphemism.

"Fuchs said in his review Gina played the Mozart like she'd slept with somebody to get the part."

I'd been amazed the paper even printed that, and I guessed that Gina, a full-blooded Italian Girl with the ripe body and hot temper to match, went off like Vesuvius when she read it. Grant was just as tacky about Dani and her Benny Goodman performance. He went after Stew's program selection, too: Mozart, Benny Goodman, a bunch of pop hits, ending with an amazing arrangement of Queen's "Bohemian Rhapsody." It brought the crowd to their feet, except for Grant, who thought it was a stupid choice.

I watched the concert, of course. When it was over, I heard a little girl on a blanket near me tell her parents she wanted to play music when she grew up. If the concert made kids feel like that, Stew definitely made good choices.

I tried to say as little as possible, but I knew damn well when the cops left my office, they thought they had three definite suspects. Someone had attacked Grant in his back yard the same night the review appeared in the paper. Police thought he was sitting in a lawn chair and listening to his iPod. He had cocaine in his bloodstream and powder around his nostrils when his neighbor saw him lying in the grass early the next morning. The contusions on his face matched a garden spade next to him, blood on the blade, the handle wiped clean.

* * *

That night, Gina texted me and I felt her agitation through my phone. She arrived wearing khaki shorts and a button-down linen shirt, translucent enough to show she wasn't wearing a bra to contain her ripe Italian breasts.

"The cops think I killed Grant," she said, her rage a red aura around her. She had long black waves and eyes dark as her clarinet, and she brought a bottle of Chianti with her to take the edge off the evening.

"He fucked you over in his review," I said.

"He fucked me over when he married me." She sipped her wine. "He was a lousy lay. Being in bed with him made me feel like a Shubert Symphony…"

I saw the punchline coming. "Unfinished?"

She nodded and we both drank.

"Actually, his coming so fast was one of the few good things about being married to him."

I stared at her. "You're kidding, right?"

She arched her eyebrows. "Think about it, Chris. Would you want Grant's cock in you any longer than necessary?"

"I see your point."

Gina's phone erupted in "Eine Kleine Nachtmusik," Danielle's ringtone. Gina swiped her screen, and Dani's voice filled the room.

"Are you home?"

"I'm at Chris's. You sound like you need a hug, too."

"I need more than a friggin' hug." Dani sounded like she was on the edge of tears, but I couldn't tell if she was sad, furious, or both.

"Get over here," Gina said. "We'll leave the door unlocked."

"You can start without me." Dani's voice vibrated like she was holding a note on her clarinet. "But don't you dare finish."

Gina dropped her shirt on the couch and pushed down her shorts to reveal her perfectly trimmed bush. She took my hand and led me to my bedroom. "If she's home, she can be here in about fifteen minutes," she said. "That gives us time to warm up."

"Just what I was thinking." I pulled my shirt over my head and dropped it on a chair. Gina cupped her breasts and watched my face.

"You like my girls?"

"You know I do." I unbuckled my belt and bent to suck her nipples. They turned to hard little rubies under my tongue. I closed my eyes and bit them gently, one after the other and back, again and again, and she sighed.

"You know I love that."

I buried my face in her cleavage and smelled her warm woman scent, getting warmer by the minute as I got harder. She pushed down my jeans and I stepped out of them. She cupped her breasts again and wrapped them around my straining boner. I humped her chest as she closed her lips around the head of my cock. I dug my fingers into her hair and she covered my cock with saliva, then pulled back and slid me down between her tits again. She rocked against me and I closed my eyes.

"Gina, Christ…"

"I love a big cock between my tits, baby. You know that, don't you?"

Before I could answer, I heard a sigh and looked up to see Dani pulling her T-shirt over her head. She was a slim blonde with smaller tits than Gina, and when she pulled her shorts down, she displayed a tiny red thong that barely covered her fluffy little bush. She pulled the thong down and kicked it away.

"That looks so hot," she said.

"We practice duets all the time." Gina didn't miss a stroke. "Come over here and we can have a trio."

My cock felt hard as a hammer. Dani climbed onto the bed where she and I could kiss, and Gina lowered herself to cover my head with her lips. She swirled her tongue across my pee slit and my pulse jumped.

"Gina, Christ. That's so good." I sank back on the bed. Her breath tickled my navel.

"I've been putting long hard things in my mouth since I was nine, baby." She gave me a wicked smile over my throbbing cock. "That's when I started lessons."

She swirled her tongue around my head and I dug my fingers into the sheets. She took me a little deeper, then let a stream of saliva drizzle down my shaft onto my balls. She did it again and ran her tongue all the way up my shaft. Dani moved down and they took turns sucking my cock. I slid my finger into my mouth, then ran it up and down Dani's ass crack and between her thighs. She moaned and I played with her little slit and felt her juices dribble out on my finger.

Gina took me all the way in and Dani took my balls in her mouth, one after the other.

"Gkk, Gkk, Gkk…" She cupped my balls with her fingers and moved her mouth faster. I rubbed Dani's slit faster, too, and she ground her snatch against my knuckle.

"Ohhh, yeahhh…"

Her ass was smaller than Gina's, a perfect size for cupping. I slid a finger into her pussy and explored her hot little folds while her juices flowed faster and faster. I slid a second finger in, and then a third until her pussy leaked out and down my fingers. She ground against my hand and I rotated my fingers to find her G spot.

"Fuck, Chris," she gasped. "That's so good."

Gina pulled back and let more saliva roll down my shaft, then took me all the way in again until my tip bumped the back of her throat and her breath tickled my pubic hair. Her tongue stroked my shaft and I gritted my teeth to keep from blowing my load. I slid another finger into Dani's hot quim and felt her walls clench. I found that little spongy patch below her navel and she squealed.

"There, there, oh, right there!"

I pumped my hand in and out and felt her move against me. She breathed harder and faster and her hips ground back against my fingers. Gina let my cock slide out of her mouth and jacked me with one hand while she moved down and nibbled Dani's clit. The room filled with the sounds of slurping and squishing and the smell of hot wet pussy.

"I'm gonna come, Chris. I'm gonna come, I'm gonna come, I'm gonna…"

Dani arched her back and let out a shriek a second before her cunt exploded in a tidal wave of juice that soaked my hand and drizzled down my arm. Gina moved to pull her close and hold her while she shuddered on my fist and moaned out her orgasm. When she sagged back next to me on the bed, Gina turned back to me.

"I want this big hard cock in my hot tight pussy."

I slid back farther on the bed and she joined me. Dani moved behind her and buried her face in Gina's ass crack. Gina gasped and then moved up so I could kiss her. Dani ate her box lunch and played with my cock until Giua's gash dripped on my stomach, along with Dani's saliva.

"Put him in, Dani," Gina said. "Slide that hard cock into me."

Dani guided my tip between Gina's lips, and Gina slowly

straightened so her tits looked huge above me. I moved my hands up to cup them, squeezed her nipples, and watched her eyes close, the sweat pour off her face and onto her chest as she lowered herself, inch by inch, onto my hard meat stick. Her cunt was warm and tight and she eased up and down, slowly at first, then a little faster. I thrust into her and she moaned, her long hair flying around her face.

Dani watched Gina bounce on my shaft.

"That's it, Gina. Fuck that big hard cock. Take him all the way in."

Gina moved faster and my balls tightened. I knew I was almost there. I pinched Gina's nipples and thrust as hard as I could, driving my cock deep inside her. Her eyes widened.

"Shit, Chris. Oh, my gaaahhhhd!"

Her face and chest turned red and her cunt milked my cock as she shuddered. I spurted like a fire hose, filled her quivering quim with my sticky love cream. She sagged forward on my chest and we kissed. A minute later, my cock slid out, shiny with her juices and my own spunk. Dani licked my cock clean, then leaned over and lapped up Gina's cream pie as it dribbled out of her pussy lips. Gina slid off my chest and lay beside me. Dani was my other side.

"That was incredible." Gina's face and chest were still bright pink. I put my arms around both women and felt my heart slow down as the room stopped spinning. When we all were back on the same planet, I turned to Dani.

"You sounded upset on the phone."

"That asshole." Dani sat up on the bed and I admired her perky breasts. They were much smaller than Gina's, a perfect mouthful.

"Who?" Gina rolled over and rested her head on her elbow.

"Who do you think? Fuchs. The cops found my number in his contacts along with some texts from the other night."

"What night?" I stayed where I could look at both naked women on my bed.

"After the concert. He texted me he wanted to talk. I figured if he was in a good mood, maybe he'd give us a decent review for a change. I met him at his place and we…talked."

"Just talked?" Gina raised an eyebrow. "Really?"

"No, dammit, not really." Dani glared at my dick like it was all my fault. "He had a little blow, so we did a line, and he said he'd give us a good review if we did a little tit for tat."

I saw where she was going. She saw my face.

"Yeah," she said. "Or, really, blow for blow."

Gina rolled her eyes to the ceiling. "You didn't."

"Yeah, I did. It didn't last long. Well, I didn't expect it would, knowing what you told me."

"I don't believe this." I remembered reading Fuchs had coke in his bloodstream when he died. "You gave him a blow job and he still gave the concert that crappy review? Especially the two of you?"

"Well, he's always had it in for Gina, since she divorced him," Dani said. "He's always wanted to have it in me, too. So…"

I raised myself on my elbows. "And the cops found the texts on his phone, so now you're a suspect."

Dani nodded. "At least I'm in good company."

Grant Fuchs Everyone, I thought. He deserved what he got.

The women lay back on the bed for a few minutes, then Dani sat up and wrapped her hand around my soft cock. I began to get stiff, and she lowered her lips to my tip. She looked back at me and smiled.

"I was hoping you'd do that."

I moved all the way onto the bed and Dani moved between my legs to suck me. Gina moved behind her and slid her tongue into the blonde woman's crack.

Dani gasped and covered my head with her lips. I felt my pulse speed up in my cock as Dani took me deeper. Gina ran her tongue up and down between Dani's legs, down to her pussy, and back up to rim her tight little butthole. Dani sighed and drew my entire cock into her mouth until her chin brushed my balls.

Gina looked at me over Dani's slim ass. Then she moved onto the bed next to me. "Dani, eat my hot pussy."

Dani moved over to bury her face between Gina's thighs, her tight little ass waving in the air until I moved behind her and locked my hands around her waist. I slid my cock up and down her ass crack like Gina did with her tongue, then guided my swollen tip between her dripping lips and into her pleasure box. Dani moaned and pushed back against me, and Gina locked her hands in Dani's hair and pulled her face tight against her own snatch. I pumped into Dani's box and pulled her ass back against me while Gina bucked under her hot tongue.

"Yeah, baby, just like that. Make me squirt."

Hearing her talk like that made my cock hard as a crowbar and I pumped even harder, lifted Dani's ass off the bed while my balls slapped between her thighs and both women moaned and cried out with pleasure. Gina screamed and arched off the bed.

"I'm coming, Dani, I'm gonna come on your sweet face. God, it's so…"

She thrashed and shuddered and her face. Dani kept licking, then Gina rolled out of the way and Dani took her place and rolled over on her back. Gina put her dripping snatch over Dani's face and stretched down to lick her pussy.

"Fuck her, Chris," she panted. "Let me see that big cock in her hot little cunt."

I almost blew my load at the idea of it, but I guided my tip into Dani again and Gina licked my shaft every time I pulled back. Her warm breath tickled my short hairs and she played with my balls with one hand. Dani dug her fingers into Gina's ass cheeks and lapped up that dripping pussy like a kitten with a bowl of cream.

"Fuck, Dani," I panted. "Fuck, Gina." I'd never felt so aroused in my life. Well, I'd never been with two women at the same time, either. Gina squeezed my balls a little tighter.

"You feel like you're ready to shoot."

"Not yet," I grunted. I thrust even harder and faster, my balls slapping between Dani's thighs.

Dani slid a finger into Gina's tight little butt hole and she squealed.

I found Gina's tit with one hand and pinched her nipple while she kept licking both me and Dani and Dani ate her pussy and fingered her ass. It was like a race, except that we all tried to hold back and not finish. Dani rocked under both of us and I felt her rhythm speed up. That made my balls tighten.

I pumped harder and faster. Gina looked up at me. Her face glowed with sweat and her eyes looked glazed. Her lips moved and I heard her faintly say, "Now."

Then she squeezed my balls and Dani wailed her orgasm to the whole neighborhood. I pumped even harder and shot my load into Dani's love box, thrusting like a jackhammer. I pulled back and another ribbon of cream shot across Gina's face. She opened her mouth to take it all in, and Dani gave her clit one last tweak that brought her off, too. We shook and moaned for what felt like hours, then collapsed into a sweaty heap on the sticky sheets.

"That was incredible," Dani whispered. Her hair was plastered to her forehead, and her face was pink as her pussy.

"Stew would be so proud," Gina said. "All three of us finishing together, just like the Mozart."

It was the most amazing sex I'd ever had.

Eventually, we all got our heartbeats and breathing back to normal and talked about Grant Fuchs.

"I hope the cops don't think you killed him," Gina said.

"Me too," I said. "Do you have an alibi for last night?"

Dani shook her head. "I was home watching Netflix. Isn't that lame? Grant finally fucked me without even being there."

"Everyone in the symphony is pissed about his crappy review," I said. "The cops are going look at everyone."

"Especially Stew," Gina said. "He really got the worst of it."

"How about you?" Dani said to her. Gina shrugged and her breasts bounced on her chest.

"He fucked me years ago. And he was lousy. I told you that, remember?"

Eventually both women took showers and got dressed again. It was nearly 2:30 before they left. I knew I'd sleep like a baby for the next four hours. I only wished I could do it for eight.

When I stood under the shower washing off the evidence the next morning, I wondered if I'd ever have to make a choice between Gina and Dani

* * *

I sat at my computer and tried to compose a release about the tragic death of Grant Fuchs that didn't make me either laugh uproariously or want to throw up. The longer I struggled for something nice to say, the more I realized that he was a loathsome excuse for a human being. I wondered how he'd managed to persuade Gina to marry him. Whatever it was, it didn't work for long. They were married less than a year.

He had a house and he paid alimony, but I wondered if he had a current—well, recent—girlfriend. He managed to get together with Danielle, so it was a safe bet he wasn't living with someone else.

Dani was furious about his suckering her—bad choice of words, there—and still trashing both her and Gina in his review. I knew Stew was livid about it, too. The police had found Dani's texts and were already looking at her. She said she'd been home alone. No alibi.

Did Gina have an alibi? Did Stew? How many other people were the cops looking at? The Symphony had about 100 musicians, and I didn't even know how many painters Grant had insulted in his reviews. Or how many local theater productions he panned. He probably hated Shakespeare, Lin-Manuel Miranda, and everyone in between.

The town was better off without him. No two ways about it.

I remembered the little girl who said she wanted to be a musician. Could I possibly track down the kid and her parents and do an article for the website? I didn't even have a picture of the kid, so it would be like finding a penny in a wheat field.

The feel of Gina's and Danielle's lips came back to me. Years of clarinet, strong lips and tongue. Oh, yes…

Detectives Winthrop and Symington appeared in my doorway again.

"Busy, Mr. Trask?"

"Uh, not really."

Winthrop walked like his feet hurt and Symington had less bounce than the day before. Well, Riverton had about one murder a year, and Fuchs was well-known, even if everyone did hate him. These guys were under some pressure to solve the case.

"We've talked to a few more people," Winthrop said. "Looks like you were right when you said Fuchs was the most unpopular man in town."

"We should have given him a medal," I said. "Or maybe a bell so people could hear him coming." Coming may have been a bad word choice, all things considered.

They almost smiled. Winthrop leaned against the wall next to the door and Symington moved over near my filing cabinet. It wasn't even noon, and they already looked sweaty and tired.

"We talked to Danielle LaFreniere yesterday afternoon," Winthrop said. "You know her well?"

"We see each other off and on," I said. "I guess you could say we're pretty good friends."

"Right. Well, we found some texts on her phone, between her and Fuchs. They sound a little spicy, and we wondered if you knew of anything between the two of them."

My armpits felt damp. I tried to keep my voice casual when I answered.

"Dani's young, smart, and attractive. Fuchs tore her performance apart in that Symphony review the other night. If they had anything going, that probably stopped it in its tracks."

"That's kind of what we thought, too. Ms. LaFreniere told us she, uh, met with the guy after the concert. She wanted to persuade him to give the symphony a decent review. She and the other clarinetist—Gina Bonadetta—are good friends. She likes Stewart Crenshaw, the new conductor. She was worried Fuchs would torpedo them."

Winthrop shifted his weight to the other foot.

"We talked to Ms. Bonadetta, too, of course. She told us Fuchs probably gave her that review because he was still pissed about the divorce, even though it was a few years ago. She didn't have a lot of fond memories of him."

"I don't think anyone did."

"No, we figure if there's a memorial service for the guy, it will turn into a roast."

"So you've got a truckload of suspects," I said. "Dozens of people who'd like to see him dead."

"Well, yeah, but we caught a lucky break last night."

Winthrop's posture didn't change, but I felt the energy in the room shift.

"Oh?'

Winthrop nodded.

"A neighbor, he lives behind Fuchs, he's got a vegetable garden, and animals have been getting into it. Or kids. Anyway, he set up a camera. It's high on the corner of his house, and it shows the garden, and the angle picks up most of Fuchs' back yard, too."

"Really."

"Uh-huh."

Symington stood straighter like he'd caught his second wind and Winthrop seemed to expect me to say something, but I didn't.

"See, that neighbor didn't check his video until late yesterday afternoon. He's the same one who saw Fuchs dead in the yard, and things got so crazy he didn't get around to it before. Well, you can see how that would go, right?"

I nodded again.

"Anyway, he turns the camera on when it gets dark, and this morning, he was fast-forwarding through it and he saw something moving around ten that night. He went back and looked at it again, and it was someone in the back yard with Fuchs. It's kind of dark, but you can tell that it's another man, and there's an argument. The other guy's pacing around in front of Fuchs' lawn chair, and they're both pretty heated. Arms waving, lots of finger-pointing, stuff like that."

My throat felt dry. I tried to gather saliva in my mouth to say something, but Winthrop kept talking.

"Finally, Fuchs stood up and got close to the guy. He pushed him, and the other man pushed him back. He stumbled over near his own flower patch by the garage, and he had a garden spade stuck in the dirt there. He grabbed it and went after the other man, but that man got it away from him and hit him with it. One time, in the face."

I heard voices down the hall, someone at the water cooler, someone else probably by the bulletin board. The elevator door hummed open and people got out. Winthrop leaned against the file cabinet.

"We looked at the video."

The floor was sinking under me. I tried to say something again, but I couldn't make my mouth work.

"You bent down and saw he was dead, then you wiped the shovel's handle with your shirt tail, trotted back to the front of the house, out of camera range. Like I said, it was about ten o'clock, give or take a few minutes."

Both detectives waited for me to say something, but I still couldn't. I thought I was going to throw up.

"It's self-defense, Mr. Trask. He was on cocaine, so he lost his temper. It was his shovel, and he tried to hit you first. Worst case, the D. A. might go for manslaughter. With a confession and a good lawyer, you could be out of jail again in a year or two. If a lawyer can sell self-defense, you might not serve any time at all."

* * *

My lawyer cut a deal with the prosecutor. I'm going to serve eighteen months for manslaughter.

The good news is that, when I get out, two beautiful women will be waiting.

Last Ride of the Valkyries
Wendy Harrison

The sound of musicians tuning their instruments echoed around the empty seats in the auditorium. It was five days before the holiday concert, the highlight of the 2019 season that had sold out early. Conductor Val Hall paced across the stage, stared at each of the players, and wondered if they were up to the challenge he had set for them. The Porta Larga Symphony Orchestra was, after all, semi-professional at best. Tackling "Die Walkure" from Wagner's Ring Cycle was at the outer limits of what most of them could manage, and well past those limits for the rest. Too late for second thoughts. He stepped up to the podium and tapped his baton. A few of them looked at him and began to shush the others.

He looked at the brass section. "Where's Siggy?" Then at the violins. "And Rochelle?" There was uncomfortable shifting in the folding chairs. His voice rose. "Anyone?"

There was a noise from the wings. A woman shrieked, "Who is she? Who're you sticking it in now? You can't do this to me."

The man's voice was softer but carried to the stage. "Rochelle. Just stop. We had our fun. It's over." A man stepped out from the side curtain, carrying a clarinet. Siggy was tall, fit, movie star handsome. Just behind him, a violin in her right hand, and brushing tears from her cheeks with her left was a woman who called to Val, "Sorry, Honey, we were discussing the opening instrumentation and lost track of time." She settled into the chair just to Val's left, the first violin spot, not looking at her husband at the podium.

Siggy shrugged and ignored the silent fury directed his way. "Can we get on with it?" He spoke with the assurance of someone who was used to having his bad behavior ignored. He was the star of the orchestra, the darling of the older patrons who donated generously when he was the one who asked. What was he doing in this small Southwest Florida city? He could play rings around the other performers. To know the answer to that, you'd have to talk to the long line of conductors who refused to work with him and to cuckolded millionaires who cut off donations to one symphony after another. How the mighty have fallen is the way they would've described his fate, and with relish, but Siggy was happy where he was. Top dog in a little kennel, well paid, with no shortage of women to warm his bed at night. He didn't think about the future. He assumed he'd be able to charm his way into, or out of, whatever situation suited him. Moving on from Rochelle suited him now. She was clingy. That would never work for him. He wasn't worried about Val who didn't dare try to get rid of the one person responsible for the financial success of this season. After a long silent moment, Val raised his baton and said, "From the top." The violins were poised, and the quivering opening notes began.

Three hours later, the exhausted players packed their instruments and started to leave, but Frida Shaw, second clarinet, stayed behind. After Rochelle headed for the door, Frida asked Val for a moment to talk. "I'll be right there," he called to his wife's back. Turning to Frida, he asked, "What's up?"

Frida could see the misery on his face. She hoped he would finally listen to her. "Val, you have to let Siggy go. He's too much trouble. Everyone's upset with his carrying on." Val shook his head, but she wasn't going to give up. "It's not just the business with Rochelle. He's drinking. A lot. He picks fights with everyone."

"And you'd like first chair," Val said. His words were harsh, but his eyes were kind.

"It's no secret. I'm just as good as he is. I wouldn't leave a trail of destruction behind like he does."

Val touched her shoulder. "I'm sorry. More than you could know.

The truth is, you're not as good as he is. Almost no one is. And he's our major fundraiser. Because of him, we're able to have this space." He waved his arm. "We'll see what happens when the season is over, but I don't see any way the Board would fire him." He turned to leave. "I'm sorry, Frida. Reality sucks." He headed toward the exit at the back of the auditorium.

Frida watched him leave. "He's going to go too far," she called out to him, "and then it'll be too late."

* * *

It was after nine o'clock when Siggy walked into the Harborside Bar & Grill. He'd napped, showered, and changed into designer jeans and a pressed white shirt fresh from the dry cleaners. He liked to wear white. It showed off his tan and dark hair, made his whitened teeth sparkle.

"The usual?" Behind the bar, Pete Cross reached for a martini glass.

Siggy nodded and looked around. "It's quiet."

Shaking the silver beaker, Pete said. "Always is on Monday."

Siggy watched Pete pour his drink and add two olives and a twist of lemon, the way he liked it. Pete glanced to the other end of the bar where a lush blonde sat, staring across at Siggy. "I'm guessing that might not be true tonight." He laughed as Siggy looked over at the woman.

It didn't take long. An hour later, Siggy and "call me Hilda" were on their way to his condo, the best view of the harbor in Porta Larga. In the large living room, one wall was dominated by a complicated sound system, shelves of vinyl albums, and a delicate turntable. "You like music?" Hilda took off her silk jacket.

"I do." Siggy began to unbutton her blouse. "You're with the best clarinet player in the country."

"Really," she said, her voice skeptical.

Turning away, he pulled a hard leather case from the bottom shelf and put it on the low table in front of the couch. As he snapped it open, she saw the gleaming instrument inside.

"Can you really play this thing?" He pulled the clarinet from the case

147

along with a reed. He sucked on it, looking at her as he did. It was clear what he had in mind for the evening. Lifting the instrument to his mouth, he began to play. She didn't expect the purity and beauty of the sound. Mesmerized, she listened and swayed.

Pleased by her response, he put down the clarinet and pulled an album from the collection. "Just listen to this. That's me, right after the violins." Hilda looked at the album cover. Wagner's "Die Walkure."

"It's the best music for what I'm going to do to you," he assured her, "and what you're going to do to me."

The violins grew in volume as he pulled her to him. He nibbled her neck as his hands pulled her blouse from her shoulders. She pushed him away.

"Let me." She grabbed his shirt and tore it open, forcing the buttons out of the buttonholes. His bare chest was smooth. His nipples puckered as she leaned over and bit each of them.

"So that's how you like it." He groaned and pulled her breasts from her bra. Leaning down to reach them, he began to suck each of them, his teeth leaving them swollen. He tore off the rest of her clothing as she opened his belt and unbuttoned his pants. Impatient, he unzipped and pulled them down, stepping out of them as his hardened dick rose with relief.

The brass instruments joined the violins and as the music gained speed, he mumbled to her, "That's me playing," and pushed her to the bedroom. They landed on the king-sized bed with her straddling him. He touched her, felt her dripping wetness, and pushed his cock inside. She gasped. "You like that, don't you, bitch?" He pinched her nipples and then pulled her ass up to meet him. They rose and fell with the music. His hand moved between them and rubbed her clit as she began to moan. At last, he began to come, pulsing his hot juice into her throbbing pussy.

She rolled off and lay next to him in the sudden silence. "The music is done."

"So am I," he said, as his eyes started to close. "Shouldn't have had that last martini."

In the morning, the alarm woke him at 10:00. Siggy rolled over, and his eyes opened to daylight and an empty bed. He hadn't heard her leave but was happy not to have to deal with the awkward aftermath of a one-night encounter. When he forced himself to stand, he realized he didn't know anything about Hilda. In a panic, he ran to the living room and was relieved to see his clarinet was there, right where he'd left it, next to the case. It was the most valuable thing he owned, and the only thing he loved. Relieved, he put it into the velvet compartment with care, pushed the envelope of reeds back where it belonged, and snapped the locks shut.

When he arrived at the concert hall for practice, Siggy left his clarinet case in the room off the wings. Only the musicians had access, so it would be safe. He needed coffee and walked onto the stage to announce he would be right back. No one was in their chairs yet, and no one interrupted their conversation to acknowledge his normal inconsiderate behavior. He took his time, chatting up the barista in the coffee shop across from the hall. When he returned, half an hour had gone by, and the musicians were in their seats. Val was at the podium going over a section of the music with the violinists. Siggy went backstage. His clarinet case was where he'd left it. He was sure he'd snapped the locks, but they were open. Annoyed with himself, he carried it to his chair, wrapped his lips around a reed to prepare it, and signaled Val. He was ready.

As he joined the brass entry into the music, he began to sweat. It became harder to hold the clarinet. The sound was impossible to sustain. Val glared at him. Was he hung over? Again? Siggy's heart raced, and he couldn't catch his breath. As he slumped forward and slid to the floor, the clarinet fell beside him.

Val jumped off the podium and rushed to Siggy. "Call 9-1-1!" Siggy wasn't breathing, so Val began CPR. Rochelle screamed, and between compressions, he yelled, "Someone shut her up!"

Frida ran to Rochelle. "Stop it." She shook her, but when the screeching didn't stop, Frida slapped Rochelle's face. Rochelle stared, shocked into silence.

"I've always wanted to do that," Frida said.

The EMTs arrived within minutes and checked Siggy. One of them looked at Val and shook his head. "We'll have to call the medical examiner," he said "and the cops. Probably a heart attack but this guy looks too young and healthy to be sure." He pulled out his cellphone.

"How long will it take?" Val looked around at the wreckage of the rehearsal.

The EMT shrugged. "As long as it takes. Could be hours. Depends on how busy Frank is. Frank Kronos. The M.E. Cops should be here soon."

* * *

I was having a bad day, which was nothing new. As the only female detective on the Porta Larga police force, I often found myself assigned to the least interesting or most dangerous cases. Brian Thorwald, my chief, was doing his best to force me out, either through boredom or serious bodily injury. The City Council had ordered him to promote a woman to detective. The local journalists were hot on the trail of sex discrimination, and politicians worried about the next election. I was the only woman who qualified, which isn't saying much since there were only two women on the force and the other one was out on maternity leave. When the chief told me to head to the Porta Larga Symphony, my first reaction was to wonder if someone's lost cat had wandered into the auditorium. The Chief said someone had died of a heart attack but an EMT with a good imagination talked Frank Kronos, the medical examiner, into doing an autopsy. "Just talk to the folks there. It won't be anything, but the mayor's wife is on the symphony board so he takes an interest. We need to make it look like we care."

* * *

I walked into the shiny new auditorium and down the aisle to the stage. It wasn't hard to see where Siggy had collapsed. Chairs were overturned, and sheet music was scattered over the floor. When I called out, "Anyone here?" a figure rose from behind the podium.

"Yes?"

I introduced myself. "And you are?"

"Val Hall. I'm the conductor." He walked toward me. "Please. Let's sit. This has been very upsetting." Gesturing toward the front row seats, he collapsed into one of them with a deep groan. I stood in front of him.

"Can you tell me what happened?"

Val described Siggy's collapse. "I gave him CPR. I took a class when I became conductor. Just a precaution. This was the first time I had to use it." He sounded exhausted. "Not that it did any good. They said it was his heart."

"Was the medical examiner here?"

Val nodded. "They said they'd take Siggy to the morgue for an autopsy, but they seemed to think it was his heart." He didn't specify who "they" was. Curious how he repeated 'it was his heart'.

I wondered how long it had taken the chief to get around to sending me here. The M.E. didn't move that fast. I asked the usual questions about whether Siggy had any enemies, any particular friends in the orchestra, any health issues.

"He wasn't very well-liked. Too much ego there. Not that I want to speak ill of the dead, but he pissed off pretty much everyone. Really, the only one he seemed to get along with was Larry Poland. The percussionist. They went out for drinks after rehearsals sometimes."

"Is he around?"

"I think he's still backstage. Everyone else left." He agreed to provide me with a list of the people who were there when Siggy collapsed. I headed to the space behind the stage. I found a hallway and several rooms. The door to one of them was open.

I stopped in the doorway and watched a short, slender redheaded man with a full beard pull drawers from an oak dresser and rummage through them. "Mr. Poland?" Larry Poland froze in place and turned toward the door.

"Yes?"

I introduced myself. "I understand you were a friend of Siggy Hagen?"

Poland stepped sidewards in a futile attempt to disguise what he had been doing. "I guess you could say that. We went out drinking after rehearsal sometimes. Not sure about the friend part, though. Siggy and I have known each other since high school band, went to college together. It was a real surprise when he turned up here after so long. I think I was the only one who could put up with him so, if that makes us friends, then yeah."

I glanced around the room. "Whose space is this?"

Poland shrugged. "Mostly Siggy's. The rest of us shared the other dressing rooms. Siggy took this one for himself."

I looked at the dresser he had been searching. A green vase, full of colorful flowers, sat on top, the only color in the room. "Nice flowers."

"From Rochelle's garden. Val Hall's wife. She hasn't been very subtle about her relationship with Siggy." He seemed eager to get me off track, but it didn't work.

"What were you looking for?"

Poland hesitated. "His clarinet. It's valuable and it isn't out in the hall. I didn't want anything to happen to it."

"That's nice of you." He stared at me to see if I was being sarcastic but gave up trying to figure it out.

"And did you find it?"

He shook his head. "No. I didn't. Maybe someone took it for safekeeping." He didn't sound as if he believed it.

"When was the last time you and Siggy went drinking?"

He thought for a moment. "Two nights ago. He seemed his usual self. The conversation was all about him. And women."

"Any women in particular? From his past maybe?"

"The closest he ever came to a real relationship was someone he dated in college. But that ended badly. She caught him cheating and ended up killing herself. Charlotte. Charlotte Brune. Real nice girl. It was a shame. Since then, Siggy's been a specialist in one-night stands.

You might want to ask Rochelle." He described the screaming match before rehearsal began. "I don't know why Val hasn't killed him." His face turned red. "I didn't mean it that way. Val wouldn't do anything like that. It was a heart attack anyway, wasn't it?"

I didn't answer. "Where did you two drink?"

"The Lighthouse mostly. It's so close, we all used to hang out there."

I told him I might have more questions for him later. Turning to leave, I suggested he lock up the room and leave with me. "No locks," he said and followed me out to the auditorium.

The Lighthouse was two blocks away from the symphony. It was past five o'clock and the bar was noisy and full. It looked like the locals used it for a break between work and home. I squeezed through the crowd to the bar and held up my ID for the bartender. "Is this about Siggy?" he asked.

"Can we talk somewhere quiet?"

The bartender turned to a woman who was pulling beer from an ice chest under the bar.

"Watch the bar for me." He motioned for me to follow. We walked to a hallway off the side of the bar and into a small office. The bartender sat behind the desk. "I'm Pete Cross."

"Detective Berta Wotan. I understand Siggy Hagen was a regular here." He nodded. "When was he here last?"

"Last night. We talked about how quiet the place always is on Monday night."

"Did he talk to anyone while he was here?"

"A little. But it was enough. He left with a blonde."

"Do you know her name?"

He shook his head. "I did hear him call her Hilda, but I've never seen her before."

"Last name?"

"Sorry. I don't think Siggy knew her. It was like him, to just pick up a stranger and take her back to his place."

I asked a few more questions but he didn't have anything helpful to say. Handing him my card, I told him to call if he saw the woman again.

From my car, I called the station and told the chief I needed a CSI team to meet me at Siggy's apartment. "What're you talking about? I send you out for a heart attack and you need CSI?" I brought him up to date and reminded him the case was of interest to the mayor. "All right. All right. Gimme the address."

I wasn't surprised I arrived at the apartment before CSI. The chief was probably going to slow roll any request I made. He'd made it clear he wasn't going to accept a woman in his squad and, mayor or no mayor, he wouldn't make things easier for me. He was just waiting for an excuse to boot me for incompetence.

The doorman let me into Siggy's place. It looked like a glossy magazine's idea of a bachelor pad. Leather, steel, black and white. I pulled on latex gloves and walked through the rooms, careful not to touch anything that might have fingerprints that could help identify the mysterious Hilda, the last person known to have seen Siggy before he arrived at rehearsal. I kept my eyes open for the missing clarinet. I couldn't exclude theft as a motive. When CSI arrived, I explained food would need to go to the lab to be tested and said to take the sheets to check for DNA that didn't match Siggy's. I noticed a turntable with a record on it and had them check for prints. When they were done, I turned it on and placed the needle on the vinyl. The music filled the room, quivering violins followed by galloping brass. Everyone stopped and listened to the end. "Man, I could use that on my next date," one of the men joked and everyone laughed.

* * *

The M.E. put a rush on the tox screen thanks to the mayor's interest. When he got the results, Frank called. "The EMT was right to call me on this one. The vic died of aconitine poisoning. It's fast and wouldn't have been picked up in the usual tox screen. Looks like a heart attack."

"What's aconitine?" I'd never heard of it.

"It's from a plant. Usually, monkshood or wolfsbane. Nasty stuff. No antidote."

"Where would someone get it?"

"They could grow it. Gardeners have been known to have poison gardens, with all kinds of lethal plants."

"In the name of all that's holy. Why would that be legal?"

"How should I know? You're the cop. Just look for someone with dirt under their nails." He hung up before I could come up with a snappy answer.

Back to the basics. I had enough suspects from the orchestra to keep me busy. If none of them panned out, I'd look further out. A case like this should have a full team on it, but the chief was looking for me to fall on my ass. I'd have to solve it before he had a chance to take it away from me.

I made a list. Means, motive, and opportunity. There was motive aplenty. Jealousy: Val Hall. Greed/ambition: Frieda Logan. Revenge: Rochelle Hall. There was also the mystery woman, Hilda, if that even was her name. No known motive at this point. Larry Poland, who showed a serious interest in the missing clarinet or whatever else he looked for in the dressing room.

It was a good decision to interview Rochelle Hall and Val Hall separately. Neither had anything good to say about the late, unlamented clarinetist. Rochelle's bitterness over their public breakup omitted any reference to the fact she was married and conducting an affair under the baton of her husband. When I moved on to Val, he stressed Siggy's importance to the orchestra's survival but couldn't hide his anger at the humiliation he had suffered.

Both Halls asked the same question. "Have you talked to Frieda Shaw?" Both gave the same reason. Frieda was desperate to be named first chair, a steppingstone to a bigger, professional orchestra.

"Desperate enough to kill him for it?" They both thought she could be. Val related his conversation with Frieda the day before Siggy died.

"It sounded like a threat to me. I didn't take it seriously. I had too much else to worry about." I assumed he referred to the scene with Siggy and his wife. "But who knows?"

I tried to decide if I had enough for a search warrant for the couple's house. The clarinet might be missing because it was a valuable instrument, according to everyone I spoke to. I'd like to get my hands on the reeds in the case. As far as I could tell, they would be the likeliest delivery system for the poison based on Frank's description of how quickly it worked. My cellphone rang as I concluded there wasn't a judge friendly enough to give me a warrant with what I had found so far.

"Detective? It's Pete, at The Lighthouse?"

"How can I help you?"

"She's here. The woman I told you about. Hilda? She's back."

I told him I'd be right there and if the woman started to leave, for him to try to keep her with an offer of another drink on the house. "I'll pay for it," I said as I grabbed my keys and ran to my car.

At The Lighthouse, I took a deep breath at the door, to calm myself, and to not spook the woman. When I walked up to the bar, Pete nodded at a woman alone to his right. Hilda was an attractive blonde with long hair in a braid down her back. She was in her late 30's, I guessed, and slim with the look of a runner.

"Hilda?"

The woman turned toward me. "Yes?"

"Detective Berta Wotan. I'd like to talk to you about Siggy Hagen." Hilda nodded as if she'd expected me. "Do you think you could come with me to the station to answer some questions?' When the woman stood, I asked if I could see identification. The woman pulled out her driver's license. "Clotilde Brune." A Tampa address.

I took a chance and seated Hilda in the passenger seat of my unmarked car. I trusted my instincts the woman not only wasn't a threat to me but wanted to talk. At the station, I stopped to get coffee for both of us and then we went into an interrogation room. I started the recording equipment.

"You're not under arrest, Ms. Brune," I told Hilda. "You're free to leave at any time. Do you understand?"

"Yes. I need to tell someone. I'm so ashamed. I wanted him dead. Siggy. I wanted to kill him."

I held up her hand to stop her. "Stop. I'm going to have to read you your rights." When I was finished, I asked, "Do you understand?"

"I do."

"Do you still want to talk to me, Ms. Brune?"

"Sure. Please call me Chloe. No one ever used Clotilde. My parents never did say how they came up with it."

"Let's start with how you knew Siggy."

Chloe explained he had dated her big sister Charlotte in college. I knew the name Brune was familiar. Larry Poland had mentioned the suicide of Charlotte Brune as the reason Siggy stuck to short-term relationships.

"I know what happened to your sister," I said. "That was twenty years ago, wasn't it?" Chloe nodded. "Why now?"

"I saw the story about him coming to Porta Larga. It all came rushing back."

"You decided to pick him up at the bar?"

"I was sure he hadn't changed. It was easy."

"Then what were you going to do?"

"Shoot him." She reached into the large purse she had put on the table.

I jumped to my feet, furious I hadn't searched Chloe when we got to the station. "Stop. Slide the purse to me."

"I didn't do it. I just couldn't."

I reached into the bag and pulled out a rusty old revolver. It wasn't going to hurt anyone in the condition it was in. It wouldn't even fire. "Where did you get this?"

"It belonged to my grandfather. I don't even know if it has bullets in it. I was so angry. I wasn't thinking straight."

"What happened at the apartment?"

Chloe looked down at her clasped hands. "It's hard to explain. He played for me. The clarinet? I've never heard anything like it. It was so pure. So beautiful. So…seductive. I'd had too much to drink, but that's not much of an excuse for what I did. I realized I'm no better than he was. When he fell asleep, I got dressed and left. I couldn't believe it when I heard the news."

"Did you touch the clarinet or the case?" She shook her head. "Or the reeds?"

"No. Siggy did when he played but not me."

"Have you gone to the symphony hall at any time?"

"No. I didn't want to see him again." I'd have her fingerprinted and make sure there were no matches to anything at the hall, but I believed her. Now I was back where I started. I decided to take another run at the Halls in the morning. Maybe they'd worked together to get rid of Siggy, or maybe they'd turn on each other and I'd find out which of them did it.

After breakfast, I called the symphony office and asked for Val. "I'm sorry." It was a woman, and she sounded as if she meant it. "They're all in a meeting." Her voice caught. I hoped she wasn't one of Siggy's playthings. She sounded so young.

"Rochelle too?"

"All of them. They're trying to figure out what to do about the concert. They'll probably be there all morning at least. Can I take a message?"

I thanked her and said I'd try later. The address I had for the Halls was on the outskirts of the downtown area, in a historic district of renovated, well-maintained old houses. I parked near their house and went through the front gate, which was set in a white picket fence. It clashed with my observations of their marriage. Technically, I was probably trespassing, but if I was lucky, no one would find out I was poking around. I didn't know what I was looking for. Some kind of clue, but since I couldn't break in, it was probably a waste of time.

The house was a two-story wood structure, painted dark green with light green trim. The front yard contained a lush garden of colorful flowers, like the ones in Siggy's dressing room. I walked along a path at the side of the house and into the backyard. It was large with freshly mowed grass and, at the far end, there was a small greenhouse. I couldn't resist. As a person with no ability to keep plants alive, I'd always fantasized if I only had a greenhouse, my world would be filled with a constant supply of flowers and vegetables. I have an infinite capacity for self-delusion.

I approached the door to the greenhouse, not to go inside without a warrant, of course, but maybe to peek through the windows, having taken the precaution of looking up photos of monkshood and wolfsbane. It was hard to imagine how any detecting got done back in the pre-Google days. There was a disturbed area of dirt adjacent to the greenhouse and a shovel a few yards away. Someone had been digging recently. It was raw, especially compared to the bright green grass everywhere else. I started carefully moving the dirt aside with my bare hands. A shadow appeared next to mine on the ground, and I rolled to the side as a pipe crashed into the ground where my head had been.

I couldn't reach my gun from the position I was in but squinted up into the sun. A woman was silhouetted against the bright light. "Rochelle?" As her arm reached for the pipe to try again, I squirmed sidewards and kicked straight up, as hard as I could. A man would've been totally disabled but Rochelle barely slowed down. Her face was distorted with rage, her eyes darted back and forth. I wasn't sure she even knew who she was trying to kill.

I managed to get off the ground and put her in a headlock. Not a legal police maneuver but it did the trick. She gagged and then slumped against me. There was no fight left in her.

I put her in cuffs and sat her on the ground. As she leaned back against the greenhouse and sobbed, I read her Miranda rights. Turning back to the small burial spot, I knew what I would find. Around six inches down, the clarinet case sat firmly inside the hole. Pulling out my phone, I called the chief.

"You won't have to worry about the mayor anymore," I said. "I arrested the murderer of Siggy Hagen. You might want to watch for my press conference. I'm going to make sure I get the credit for solving the case. Then I'm going to quit. Explain that to the mayor, why don't you?"

Rescue Me
Sandra Murphy

Dave looked around the hotel room. As hotels go, it was pretty nice, a well-stocked mini bar, some plants, artwork he'd bet wasn't the same in every room, and a bed big enough to host an orgy. Not that there was much chance of that happening. He sighed and looked at the round table near the window. Covered in loose papers, a ledger, lists, and a mug filled with pencils, it looked like gibberish and junk. Might as well sort through it. Not as much fun as the porn channel but something to do.

Invoices in one stack, receivables in another, he'd just reached for the lists when a sound at the door made him notice the knob turning.

Before he could stand up, a tall woman wearing a long red dress, slit up the side, and glittery spike heels slipped into the room. The door had barely closed when she pushed in the button lock, flipped the deadbolt, and latched the safety bar. With a deep sigh, she slumped against the door, still facing away from him.

"I think you have the wrong room," Dave said. Barefooted, he'd made no sound on the plush carpet.

She jumped back, fumbled for the doorknob, "I thought, I had to, I didn't know…"

"Guess you didn't see me." Dave spoke softly. He didn't need a woman screaming for help in his locked hotel room. At least he was dressed. Half an hour earlier, and she'd have caught him walking around naked, post-shower, dick in his hand. "What's wrong?"

"Two men, they're after me." Her head turned side to side, looking for an escape. "They want to kill me. I saw something I shouldn't have.

Please, don't let them find me!"

As she turned, her hand clutched the fabric over her left breast, or is that boob or titty? Maybe he shouldn't mention it. Whatever it was called, there was a lot more of it than fit in her hand.

She didn't seem to notice as if her fingers rolled over the fabric on their own. Even through the red silk, he could see her perky nipple. For himself, all he could say was his erection was getting hard. And even harder to ignore.

"What men? What did you see?"

"I was serving drinks." She listened at the door. "I should go, I can't put you in danger too." Her left hand never stopped moving.

Dave looked out the peephole. "Were they wearing black? One's bald?"

"Damn, my dress is torn, fabric's missing. It must have gotten caught on the door. They'll see it and know I'm here!" Her desperation grew. "Fuck, fuck, fuck, the bathroom's too obvious, the bed's a platform, can't get under it."

"There's a screen back there in the corner, behind the plants. Go, duck down, hide. Hurry!"

A fist pounded on the door. "Hang on a minute," Dave called. He clicked the remote for the 48" television, unbuttoned his shirt, pulled most of it out of his jeans, and hoped the flopping fabric would hide his overexcited cock. As he walked to the door, he mussed his hair and undid the snap at his waistband, slid the zipper down an inch, then two. Phone in hand, he spoke softly.

He leaned against the frame, half behind the door, his left foot firmly planted over the missing piece of fabric. "What's all the racket about, fellas?"

"We're looking for, uh, our friend." One of the men scanned the hallway while the other talked. "She wanders off, gets too friendly with men she doesn't know."

Dave scratched himself and said, "Dude, if she was in here, I wouldn't be talking to you, I'd be doin' the nasty. Did you know channel sixty-nine is all-porn, all the time? I was in the middle of a hot fantasy, banging a chick with big tits when you started banging the door. Get it? Banging the door?" In the background, channel 69 provided breathy and grunting sound effects that explained the bulge in Dave's jeans.

"The boss'll kill us for losing her." Baldy tried to look into the room.

"Just how friendly is she? I mean, send her my way and I'll give you a hundred bucks if she likes to suck cock. Two, for a good long fuck." Dave rubbed his growing bulge.

He looked over Baldy's shoulder. "Hey, is the elevator coming?"

A ding followed by elevator doors opening sent one man running. The other yelled, "I'll clear out the room in case she called the cops. You find her and shut her up! Permanently!"

Dave slammed and locked the door. "They're gone. You're safe now."

"Are you sure? What luck the elevator came."

Dave held up his cell phone and said, "Alice, play ding and door sounds." He grinned. "Comes any time I want."

"Coming any time you want is a handy skill to have." She walked to him, standing close enough he was sure his shirttail wasn't going to be able to hide anything as big as his dick felt. She reached for his hand and fabric fell forward, the strap ripped loose, exposing her breast, nipple at attention. She put the heel of his hand high on her ribcage, his fingers where hers had been, her nipple between his first and middle fingers. "You deserve a reward, you saved me." Her hand over his, gently squeezed. "Feel how hard my heart is pumping, throbbing. Can you feel it?"

"Oh yeah, feeling it, sure am," Dave gasped. Oh god, now what? He felt like a grenade was about to explode in his jeans. Think about something else! "What did you see?"

"They played cards, then said I could leave. I went into the bathroom to freshen up and when I came, out into the room again, there was a third man. Pills, all over the table. A briefcase full of money. One of them saw me, grabbed for me, tore my dress. I ran." She looked up at

Dave's face. "I should go. I interrupted you. I don't want you to be…frustrated." She brushed her right hand down the front of his jeans, flexed his hand on her tit. "Or maybe you believed them, that I'm easy, will fuck anybody."

"No, really, I can tell you're not like that. Stay." Dave looked at her dress. "You really can't go out anyway. That uh, part where the slit is in your skirt is torn. You kind of flashed me with every step you took, coming, uh, walking I mean, over here."

"You could see I'm not wearing panties? Damn Suzie. This was her job. It'll be easy, she said, serve a few drinks." She examined the dress, revealing more than Dave had seen before, his hand still on her boob. "I should have known better. Suzie calls this her Tits for Tips dress because it's so low cut and the slit goes so high. She's getting off in the Bahamas, fucking her pencil dick boyfriend, probably coming every five minutes. I got stiffed on tips."

She looked down. "Speaking of stiff... what you said?"

"I thought gross would get rid of them. No disrespect to you."

"Because I was thinking, if it's not an imposition I mean, all that bending over, leaning forward, and being chased, it was scary but exciting. Could you give me a little rubdown, so I could relax?" She stepped closer. "Or you could keep me company while I relax myself. I just don't want to do it alone."

"Uh, oh yeah, I'd be happy to, whatever you want." Dave gulped as her hand went to his zipper and stroked the denim.

As she stepped back, the other strap on her dress slipped. The fabric slid over her right breast, hesitated as it caught briefly on the erect nipple, and then in agonizingly slow motion, continued down her body, to fall into a silken puddle at her feet. She slid the shirt off his shoulders and dropped it to the floor. "Chest hair, just the right amount to tickle and arouse." She ran her hands over his muscles. "You should get out of those jeans. They've gotten about four sizes too small in the last few minutes." She tugged the zipper and Dave hoped he wouldn't come right in her hand.

She led him by his dick to the bed and pillows high behind her shoulders, stretched out, legs spread wide. "When I'm alone, it's so much harder. I have toys but it's not the same as feeling the weight of a man's powerful dick, hearing the sounds he makes as he goes deeper with each thrust." She massaged and licked her nipples. "I wish I could show you the difference."

"Um, I checked the bedside drawer there, looking for a pen. This is some full-service hotel. There's a vibrator in there, still in the plastic wrap." Dave had his dick in hand, ready if needed.

"Only six inches long and an inch around, it's shorter and not nearly as filling as your cock would be," she said. Her fingers slid between her legs. "It's hard to reach the best places. I like the buzzy feeling but using it, I can only touch and lick one titty. I like both at the same time. You should remember that."

Dave nodded so hard that his dick nodded too.

She slid the vibrator between her legs, turned it on low, then adjusted it to medium. "If you'd like to kiss and lick me, you could start at the arches of my feet, alternating legs on your way up. Make it last, but don't keep me waiting too long. I don't want to come without you."

Dave willed his dick to think of baseball scores as he kissed her arch, the curve near her heel and licked his way to the dimple of her knee, eyes on the vibrator as it slid in and out of his destination.

"I want your tongue to tickle me, to feel your fingers inside."

Within seconds, Dave's tongue danced between her legs, three fingers slid in and out as she moaned. "Oh, I can't wait, I want to come, make me come, harder, faster, oh oh, oh, I'm coming." She writhed under his thrusting fingers and speeding tongue. His dick rubbed against the soft bedclothes but held steady. She seemed to come forever.

"Oh my god, it's never been like that before." She could hardly breathe. "I came six times before I lost count."

Dave moved into fucking position but she had other ideas. "I want to ride your cock." She pushed it flat against his stomach and straddled him. Back and forth, she slid far enough over the tip to rub herself against his belly hair. "Ooh, that's what I like, the feel of a huge dick between my legs. My boobs, suck, lick, both at once."

She began to move faster until he was sure he was going to blow it. Just in time, she stopped, eased back and let his cock stand like a flagpole. She raised herself enough to take just the tip inside. "Is this where you want to go? Where you want to come?"

He massaged her ass. "Oh yeah, I want to fuck you until you can't come any more."

"Then let the games begin," she said and slammed herself down, taking the full length of his dick inside. Before he could register how good it felt, how tight she was, she'd raised up and did it again, rocking forward just a bit.

After half a dozen times, each one being the one he was sure would be the tipping point beyond his ability to hold back, she rolled over, his dick still inside, her legs tight around his waist as she thrust herself against him. "Fuck, fuck, make me come again, again, and again." At last, his dick got its reward for waiting.

Twenty minutes later, she put his hand between her legs. "Feel how hard it's throbbing. Gimme more."

"You, missy, are greedy."

"One can never have enough fine wine, good chocolate, or put a limit to the number of times a long, thick, very hard dick slides in and out and makes me come. If the dick is big enough, and yours is, maybe I'd forget the wine and chocolate." She grinned.

"Play with your toy while you wait for me. I'll watch and learn."

"I tossed it off the bed in favor of the real thing. The battery's dead." She sighed. "I could ask a bellman to bring up batteries, lots more, explain why. I'd answer the door wearing your shirt, probably buttoned."

"Sure, torture another poor dick. Mine will need the paddles and someone yelling 'clear' to come back."

"Or mouth to mouth?" She slid down Dave's stomach. After a few minutes of tongue-to-dick therapy, she said, "I was right. Not dead, just stunned. Follow me." She took his hand. "Is this where you were working when I came…in?"

"Yeah, straightening papers somebody left." His hard cock bobbed as he walked.

She leaned over the back of the chair. "So, if I was just standing here, all naked and fuckworthy, and someone with a really big erection came up behind me, well…you could fulfill your fantasy about banging a chick with big tits. Think of people in other buildings, watching, you between my legs, my titties bouncing, until we're both screaming a climax like they've never seen or heard, not even on channel sixty-nine."

It was impossible to say if they were watched or not but the idea of an audience made him hot, made him come, harder than before. "I might make it to the bed," Dave said. "My dick's dead. I'll die happy." He collapsed into a pillow.

"Rest up." She had a quick shower. Dave was asleep when she returned.

Her lips were coated in a vibrant red, high gloss lip color. She picked up a cloth napkin, and opening her mouth wide, wide enough that a hard, thick, erect dick would fit, she blotted her lips and laid the napkin on the table next to the piece of fabric torn from her dress.

Smiling and still naked, she went to the connecting door and into the next room where the bald man waited. "I laid out a running bra and shorts for you but judging by how chapped you are, sweats would be a better idea." He handed her a small tube. "I brought salve."

"Stan, I did him so many times, he's in a come coma. He was a good fuck so I kept going. Or should I say coming? The rescue fantasy's a classic. He paid when he booked, no quibbling, added a nice tip." She handed Stan the torn dress and sparkly shoes. "Gimme my clothes and let's get out of here. Thursday evening we've got the symphony guy, the one who likes to lick body-painted musical notes off me. Painting them on takes longer to do than licking them off."

"He's the one who bangs the cymbals at the climax?" Stan laughed.

"And then he goes to work?"

"That wasn't funny last week and still isn't. Who's cooking tonight, me or you?"

"Sweetie, cooking's not part of my job description but your efforts are just not edible. Let's call for pizza. Running down the hall, threatening to kill you, wears me out." Stan slung an arm around her shoulders. "One movie, then I'm going back to my place to recover."

* * *

Two hours later, Dave woke up. He knew she'd be gone but his dick had hoped she'd stayed. Red and sore, it was ready to rise to the occasion once again. Once more into the breech? Or into the girl at least.

Dave absently stroked it as he walked over to the table and sat in front of the window. A spot had been cleared of papers and junk. There was a white cloth napkin with an open-mouthed imprint of red glossy lips, just the right size for a penis that loved to be sucked. Next to it was the scrap of her dress and a business card that read:

Fantasy Dates, Discreet Encounters
For the Imaginative Man.
Come, play with me.

He lifted the napkin to his face and smelled a faint hint of her perfume, tasted her scent still on his hand. Wrapping the ripped red silk around his cock, he closed his eyes, and began to stroke himself to a full erection and an explosive climax. Maybe, this time, someone was watching.

* * *

Two men painted musical notes on Dara's bare skin. "He'll be here in forty-five minutes, how much is there left to do?" she asked. "The brush tickles."

"Not much. Need to add single notes and the little signs," Stan said. "The bristles tickle because lines take less paint. Bobby, how're you doin' back there?"

"Finishing the No Entry signs." Bobby blew out a breath, his face closer to her ass than it should have been. "Why would a guy pay so much to have stuff painted on a bitch's butt? Cheaper to just get it on. Geez, a piece of ass is a piece of ass."

He'd barely finished the sentence when Dara's hand wrapped around his throat as she pushed him against the brick wall. "I am not a piece of ass. I am a fucking professional, capital F, capital P, Fucking Professional. I'm worth every penny I get paid. I don't sell myself. I rent." she said. His face was red, edging toward purple, but she ignored that. "It means my profession is fucking, however he wants it, as long as he wants it, provided it doesn't violate my rules. You have about as much talent as a pimply teenage boy ogling a Playboy centerfold, coloring the nipples with crayons, and jacking off while doing it." She let go and he slid down the wall. "Pick up your dick and leave!"

Bobby hobbled to the door.

"Dearest girl, you were a little rough on him." Stan added black body paint to his brush. "Stand in front of the air conditioner vent. You're hot and bothered enough to melt the paint. Look, puckers, just what the half notes need." He stroked paint on her nipple.

"Easy for you to say. He wasn't about to stick his thumb up your ass." She turned to the other side so he could paint a matching note on the left too.

"It was his middle finger." Stan smiled. "Big difference. Now, hold still while I clean up where your jumping around smeared the paint."

"Get the signs done." Cold lotion, used to remove the smeared paint, made Dara squirm. "Sergio insisted on coming here instead of meeting in neutral territory. Make sure that little prick Bobby didn't plant microphones or cameras."

"You got it, boss."

Twenty minutes later, Stan had cleared away his paints, reported no cameras or mics, and left for his condo next door. Just in time. Dara answered the doorman's call. "Send him up, please."

"Computer, play music mix number four." Naked, she opened the door. "Sergio, want to play me?"

Serge looked more serious than usual. Across the hall, an old man opened his door and looked out.

"Hi, Mr. Carl, how are you today?" Dara jiggled her boobs at him. The old man grinned and turned his walker around with more speed than one would expect.

"Who is he?" Serge looked toward the elevator and back.

"My neighbor. He only has dirty magazines to entertain himself." Dara closed the door and locked it. "His caregiver says he's much nicer after he sees boobs. What's wrong? I'm naked and you're not smiling."

He leaned close, nuzzled her neck, and whispered, "Serious talk. No camera, recorder?"

"No, promise. We can talk, do anything. No one sees." She unbuttoned his shirt as she whispered in return. "Tell me."

"No talking loud or facing window." He moaned as she ran her hands over his body and neared his belt buckle. "Drones. Have something for you, important."

She turned so he faced the door and she, the window. "I bet you have something for me. Come, this way." She walked him backward to the couch, unzipped his slacks, and reached inside. "I have a new paint flavor you'll like. Try the half notes." Leaning close, she put her boob near his mouth, "What is it?"

"Very bad, tomorrow, orchestra." He licked and kissed her. "I have proof to stop. I give to you, you hide, yes? Man pick up later."

"How bad?" She slid to her knees and took him between her hands, then into her mouth.

"People die, Serge too. Cooperate or they kill families." He moaned as she stopped sucking.

Instead, she straddled him. "Lick the paint."

He held her breasts. "These notes, they always play at the same time, yes?" He licked the paint and sucked her nipples. "Ah, taste is espresso, perfect!"

"What man tonight?" She stood, turned her back to him, and let him see the No Entry signs painted on her ass. "What do I hide it, how big is it?" Turning around, she pointed to the Welcome, Come on Down, Enter Here signs painted below her navel with arrows pointing to the desired destination.

He laughed. "Please, no talk now. Come to me. Let me do as signs tell me." He buried his face between her legs and got his wish. There was no more talk, only satisfied moans.

"You need a rest," Dara said. "Only a few minutes, then I want more. Come, the bed has more room to play."

He picked up his slacks and took something from his pocket before following her. "I think today, is your turn. You always give. Is now time to receive." Serge stretched out beside Dara, ran his hands over her body, lingering in the most sensitive places. "I have the concert when we shall make beautiful music. At the right moment, I pick up the large gold cymbals and when the conductor points at me, I crash them together. It is like sex, yes?"

"Very much like sex. With the music playing and your back to the window, no one can hear what we're saying. Who will come see me later? How will I know you sent him?" Dara pressed against the curve of Serge's body, feeling his hardness at the small of her back. "What will I give him?"

"This." He held what looked like a pearl attached to a ribbon with a bow on the opposite end and stroked it over her breasts. "Proof. Instead of myself inside you, I put this. He will ask what you have for him. You let him retrieve. Simple, yes?"

Dara rolled over. Her hand went naturally to hold his dick, hard and ready. "You're not giving me this? What do I get instead?"

"I think today, it goes here, until the cymbals crash." He traced his finger around her lips, over her teeth and into her mouth. "Then I should do the same for you. When all done, pearl is hidden."

"I should get busy." Her hand caressed his cock in slow motion. "I sense urgency about timing." She wriggled and turned until she was in position to watch her hand move. "Serge, take care of this. I quite like it." Her mouth replaced her hand, moving faster.

Forty-five minutes later, Serge was dressed, ready to leave. "I shall see you again, Dara."

"You'd better." She reached to open the door. "Will your friend expect the same benefits? You didn't tell me his name."

"He does not know of your work. It is up to you whether you divulge yourself or invite his attentions, as long as I am welcome to come again, like the painted sign says," Serge said with a grin. He leaned forward and kissed her, then headed out the door.

"The name?"

"Is one you will remember. Name is Dick." Serge laughed all the way to the elevator.

Mr. Carl stood in his doorway, ogling Dara's nudity.

"You're a pervert, Mr. Carl," Dara called.

The old man nodded and smiled, his hand jerking between the folds of his flannel robe.

* * *

About midnight, Alphonse, the nighttime doorman, buzzed Dara. "There's a gentleman here to see you, miss. It's kind of late."

"He's a friend of a friend. It's all right. Thank you, Alphonse."

Feeling spy-ish, Dara wore a vintage suit without a blouse beneath the jacket, seamed stockings, and added a garter belt for extra sex appeal. Three-inch heels completed the look, blood red to match the suit.

She opened the door before he could knock. By the look on his face, she wasn't what he expected. He wasn't what she had in mind either.

Tall, with a trench coat and fedora, he looked like a 40s movie character. "Hello, miss. Serge said you stay up late so I took the chance." He set his hat on the table by the door. He looked around, everywhere but at Dara.

"Please, come in. Let me take your coat." Dara hung it on the coat rack. "I have snacks, cheeses, crackers, spreads. Or something more filling, if you'd like. A drink?"

"You shouldn't have gone to any trouble, but I did miss dinner. And lunch too, I think."

"A whiskey man, am I right?"

"Yes, but Serge said he left something here for me. If it's important, I'll have to go back to the office. Coffee, if it's made. Black with two sugars?"

"Maybe next time then, for the whiskey." Dara filled a large sturdy mug.

"How do you know Serge?" He stirred sugar into the steaming coffee. He still hadn't really looked at her.

"He teaches me about music. I share a bit about painting." Dara pushed the plate of cheeses and meats closer. "That's champagne mustard in the little dish, aioli in the other. Mayo really."

"You're not eating?" He spread mustard on a small slice of rye bread, topped it with cheddar cheese and a thin slice of ham.

Dara caught herself staring at the front of his pants. She was so used to greeting men who, in anticipation, were already hard, she was disappointed to see Dick wasn't. "Uh, no. I'll nibble later."

"What is it that you do? Serge didn't say." He reached for another slice of bread. "This is really good. I guess I was hungrier than I thought." He smiled and for once, looked at her. He startled but recovered.

"People have fantasies. I turn them into reality." Dara picked up a slice of cheddar. "I find it very satisfying." Particularly when she saw Dick's eyes drift to her cleavage.

"Um, is there any more of that mustard? I seem to have eaten it all."

"Of course." Dara walked toward the kitchen. She heard his sharp intake of breath.

"You have seams on your legs. With little arrows pointing up." He took a deep breath. "Why are there arrows?"

"Because men won't ask for directions. I don't want them to get lost." Just as she leaned forward to set the mustard down, he turned, his face touching bare skin. He almost choked. "Dick's not your real name, is it?"

"Serge thinks it's funny to call me that."

Dara took pity and sat on the couch, legs crossed.

"Those are stockings, not like well, um, but real stockings."

"Yes, real stockings, held up by a garter belt. With matching tap pants and bra. Dara crossed her legs the other way. "What else do you want to know?"

"I'd better collect whatever Serge left for me before my mouth gets me in too deep." He shifted in his chair to adjust his dick now that she had its attention.

"If you want Serge's information, letting your mouth get you in deep is required." Dara stood and held out her hand. "How are you at finding hidden treasure?"

She led him to the bed, noticed how uncomfortable he was. Un-com. Not a phrase that would do, not for this night. Dara reached for his suitcoat.

"What are you doing? Is Serge playing a trick on me? This isn't why I came." He pulled as hard to keep his jacket on as she pulled to get it off.

"Listen, Dick, you haven't come yet and if you don't get that jacket and everything else off, you're not going to." She pulled his face close to hers. "Keep your voice down. Serge says drones are spying on us. You've got to make this look like a real booty call. Now, jacket off."

"Dr…" Her lips prevented him from finishing the word.

"You see that thing flying around outside the window? Drone."

"It's a bat." At least he mumbled into her hair. "My name's Mark."

"Except we don't have bats here, Mark. Except I saw it when we were in the living room. Except it followed us. Do what I tell you." This time, his jacket came off, followed by his shirt and tie.

She nuzzled his chest and whispered, "Now you take off my jacket. Look horny or at least interested. Serge says people will die, him included. That would make me unhappy." She held her face up for a kiss and received a light peck before he added enthusiasm. Dara stepped back as he unbuttoned her jacket to reveal a black lace demi bra that showed her full breasts to their best advantage. "Put on a show for whoever's watching." Dara hoped the spy was rock hard, seeing live sex. Maybe he'd get off or better yet, there'd be others nearby so he couldn't. She hoped it made his dick hurt.

"It's all covered in silver sparkles and little stars." Mark reached out with one finger to touch bare skin just above the bra's lacy trim.

"It hooks in the front so lean in, unhook it and bury your face in my boobs. Lick them, kiss them, suck them."

Dick, uh, Mark looked like he might pass out. He sat heavily on the edge of the bed but did as he was told. With increasing enthusiasm.

Dara stepped out of her skirt, then the tap pants, leaving just the garter belt and stockings. She slid to her knees and unzipped Mark's pants, reached in for his fully hard cock. "Stand up, kick those pants away, then get on the bed on your back." She fondled her boobs as he followed instructions. "Now, I'm going to put your dick in my mouth and suck on it. Whatever you do, don't come. I'll need that for after I pass you Serge's proof."

"Who? Oh, yeah, what else are we going to do? I never thought…he said just to come…I shouldn't use that word right now."

Dara grinned and holding his dick in a firm grip, she slid her hand slowly up and down while sucking on just the tip. The drone got closer to the window. She continued but maneuvered her boob closer. Looking right at the window, she took both Mark's dick and her nipple in her mouth. The sound of the drone hitting the glass almost made her laugh.

"What was that noise?" Mark jumped a bit, pushed himself deeper into her mouth.

She reluctantly pulled away, turned. crawled next to him, whispered in his ear. "That was the sound of a drone operator fucking himself while at work. Go face first between my legs. Play a bit but notice a small red bow. When I give you the signal, gently pull on it. At the other end is a pearl. That's from Serge."

"Then what? I leave?" Mark's face flashed a panicked look.

"You can't go back to the office with a big, hard dick. What would the other boys say? You'll fuck me until we both come, me multiple times." She rolled onto her back. "Then, get that information to your boss."

* * *

The 'treasure hunt' went more smoothly than expected. When Mark left, Mr. Carl was in his doorway again. She held up three fingers and put a shocked look on her face. Mr. Carl nodded and grinned so wide, she was afraid his dentures would fall out. He spun his walker around and disappeared inside.

"Does he do that all the time?"

"It's hard to get anything past Mr. Carl although sometimes I disappoint him by being dressed."

"I don't guess there'd be any vacancies on this floor, huh? Naked babes are a benefit most rental agents forget to mention."

"Sorry, no. Let me know what happens?"

"I will. Maybe I should call before coming…dang, after you tickled your tonsils with my dick, everything I say sounds dirty."

"My phone number's in your pocket. Mr. Carl will be glad you came." Dara smiled. "Better hurry."

* * *

Stan was in Dara's kitchen plating French toast, slicing bananas, and frying brown sugar bacon when the aroma woke her.

"Damn, girlfriend, I thought I'd have to fry up the whole pound of bacon before your eyelids budged. Check the headlines. Then tell me all the details about that satisfied man who was seen leaving here late last night."

"Have you been talking to Mr. Carl?" Dara opened the paper with one hand and picked up her coffee cup with the other.

"No, darling girl. Mr. Carl is not the only one who monitors the comings and goings around here. Especially the comings. Speaking of coming, you're out of bananas."

"Oh my god, there was a bomb planted at the symphony hall. It says an anonymous tip let the bomb squad find and defuse it before the concert. It was in protest of an 'unannounced honored guest' who remains anonymous." Dara flipped to page three. "When the music hit the crescendo and the cymbals crashed, it would have exploded. Holy shit, Stan, that would be Sergio!"

"Speaking of Serge, he called. He wants to give you a tour of the concert hall, something about the acoustics in the balcony. He has new music for me to paint on you. Dave rang, wants me to get a Bentley and drive the two of you around on awards night. I think he wants to do it in the back seat and use a gold vibrator shaped like a familiar statue as his backup. The glass behind the driver's seat will be one way so I don't forget I'm driving. As you and he will be so turned on, the intercom will be turned off. I expect a full report on how many orgasms you get per mile." Stan set Dara's plate in front of her. "Eat up, honey. That man from last night called and said to tell you Mr. Carl wants him to come again. Eleven o'clock. Last night was your civic duty. Shall we bill him from now on?"

"Fantasy pays well. We have enough business." Dara forked up a piece of French toast, dripping with butter and powdered sugar. "I think I deserve one pro-boner client, don't you?"

"Too early in the day for penis puns, Miss Thing. You've got butter on your titty by the way."

"Stan, I love my Fucking Job." She licked the drip of butter and powdered sugar from her nipple. "Just fucking love it."

Our Orgasmic Orchestra

Jack Bates first wrote his story featuring a seductive balaclava player. "Olga strummed her fingers over the prized balaclava, each note drawing the man to her..." He confused a balaclava, aka ski mask in the States, for a balalaika, a triangular string instrument from Russia. When he applies himself, Bates is a pretty decent writer, if he does say so himself.

Laura Hazan was published in Natural Bridge, the Strongly Worded Women anthology, and was a writer-in-residence for the Highlandtown Arts District in Baltimore, Maryland where she resides. She is a librarian but not for a symphony, although she knows a few things about tying knots. It's best not to ask for details.

Anna V. Nelson is the pen name for a published cozy mystery author, too shy and too old to write erotica under her real name. But the old lady does love the humorous and the murderous, so she has produced stories with zany protagonists such as pot-bellied pigs, guardian angels and down-on-the-farm relatives with a penchant for delivering chaotic Thanksgiving dinners.

Too much of "The Tail" is true for **Chandler Christie** to paint a target on his trench coat by spilling the details. Let's just say this San Francisco writer publishes a steady trickle of stories and novels under various names, approves of sex and violins, prefers noir to the Beats, and favors Google-bussing the tech bros to Texas or Florida.

Albert Tucher is the creator of suburban sex worker Diana Andrews, whose job gets her into many a jam, but never one she can't solve with her unique insights into human nature. Tucher lives in New Jersey and loves New Jersey Turnpike jokes.

Shari Held: Passion, desire, lust, obsession, revenge, rage. Most everyone enjoys reading stories that make their heart race—in a good way! And who doesn't delight when a heartless rogue receives his comeuppance? Shari Held doesn't mind immersing herself in research for inspiration. Kama Sutra, anyone? When she isn't researching, she writes short fiction in multiple genres. More than three dozen of her stories have appeared in magazines and anthologies.

Hot momma! Sexy babe! Cougar on the prowl! *Karen Keeley* is none of those things, but she is a storyteller. She had oodles of fun with the story submitted for Sex & Violins, and if she were those things just mentioned, she'd certainly be her protagonist. Her story "Lovely, Just Bloody Lovely", is included in *Peace, Love and Crime: Crime Fiction Inspired by the Songs of the 60s.* (Keeley is Canadian and throws in extra letters in her spelling. We humour her.)

Joseph S. Walker, an Edgar-nominated writer from Indiana, concluded his talents lay outside the world of music when nine years of piano lessons left him utterly incapable of playing a note. His character, Ruby, is a true believer in the writer's adage, show, don't tell. He has published more than eighty short stories in magazines and anthologies, including *Peace, Love and Crime: Crime Fiction Inspired by the Songs of the Sixties.*

Linda Kay Hardie writes short stories in various genres, but not romance. She tried once, and everyone ended up dead. Tragic. She also writes recipes and is the reigning Spam champion for Nevada (yes, the tasty treat of canned mystery meat). Her writing has won awards dating back to a fifth-grade essay on fire safety. Her story showcases the many uses of a cello. Linda has a master's degree in English from the University of Nevada, Reno, where she teaches required courses to unwilling students.

Steve Liskow has stories published by *Alfred Hitchcock's Mystery Magazine, Black Cat Mystery Magazine, Mystery Magazine,* and in anthologies. He has been a finalist for the Edgar Award and Shamus Award. "Reed Between the Lines" is the first erotica he has published under his real name, and he thanks several former girlfriends (including two classical musicians) for helping with his inspiration and research.

Wendy Harrison is a retired prosecutor who turned to short mystery fiction during the pandemic. Unlike in real life, all the bad guys now get their comeuppance. Her stories have been published in numerous anthologies that began with *Peace, Love, and Crime: Crime Fiction Inspired by Songs of the 60s.* They say if you remember the 60s, you weren't there. She does. And she was.

What will **Sandra Murphy**'s former teachers, friends, and family say when her bizarre sense of humor, knack for inappropriate behavior, and generally criminal tendencies catch up with her? "I said then, we never should have taught that sex ed class to impressionable children!" says Mrs. Taylor, her sixth-grade teacher. "She was easily influenced." Spoken by a friend from kindergarten who wishes to remain anonymous. "She always blamed her friends. You know, the 'friends' no one could see." It's her family's standard line for anything she ever did, all of whom would be appalled to read the story she wrote for this anthology.

www.ingramcontent.com/pod-product-compliance
Lightning Source LLC
Chambersburg PA
CBHW032308310726
48973CB00008B/2564